MW01633700

SAVING LAURA

SPECIAL FORCES: OPERATION ALPHA

KD MICHAELS

Dear Readers,

Welcome to the Special Forces: Operation Alpha Fan-Fiction world!

If you are new to this amazing world, in a nutshell the author wrote a story using one or more of my characters in it. Sometimes that character has a major role in the story, and other times they are only mentioned briefly. This is perfectly legal and allowable because they are going through Aces Press to publish the story.

This book is entirely the work of the author who wrote it. While I might have assisted with brainstorming and other ideas about which of my characters to use, I didn't have any part in the process or writing or editing the story.

I'm proud and excited that so many authors loved my characters enough that they wanted to write them into their own story. Thank you for supporting them, and me!

READ ON!
Xoxo
Susan Stoker

ACKNOWLEDGMENTS

A huge thank you to Susan Stoker for taking a chance on me and allowing me to be a part of your Special Ops World, listening to me worry about the story and genuinely being there for me as a new author. I am truly blessed to know you.

To Sandra Sasser and to Ruth Elaine Kriss for being my cheerleaders and kicking me in the rear when I wanted to give up thinking I wasn't good enough for this ride. Thank you for being my ears, my motivators and for being friends.

To GiGi Hoggard for being the most amazing photographer, listening to my crazy ideas and taking it all in stride and being a friend. Love you suga.

To Loredana Schwartz for taking on my edits last minute and for listening to me talk about all my edits and what I truly wanted out of the story and not knowing how to get that story out there. Thank you for taking a chance on my being new.

To LeTeisha Newton, THANK YOU THANK YOU THANK YOU for my amazing book cover and assisting me in finding my way.

To Wren Michaels, thank you for being the sweetie you are and talking to me and not laughing at me with all my crazy questions.

Last but not least, my son Donald and my daughter Kimberly. Thanks for not laughing at your mom when she told you she was finally going to put her work out there for others to see. I'm blessed to have you two as children, even when you make me want to feed you to the sharks. I love you bunches!!!

1

———

Lt. Joe 'Highlander' MacLeod walked into the kitchen after getting cleaned up from his morning run and saw his fiancée, Laura 'Red' Pratt at the stove making their breakfast of eggs and bacon. The table had already been set up so he went to the fridge to grab the juice, poured each of them a glass, and set them on the table. When he got home early this morning, she was already in bed and sound asleep. He didn't have the heart to wake her up, even though he hadn't seen her in two weeks, thanks to his last mission. Joe walked up behind her, wrapping his arms around her waist, and inhaled her scent as she leaned back into him.

Holding her close, he was truly amazed they had made it this far together. Between both their careers, his as a SEAL for the US Navy and hers as a Detective for a Special Task Force for the Riverton County Sheriff's Department, most didn't think they would last a year. But they did and they were just as madly in love with each other today as they were the day they decided to admit their feelings and take the next step. Joe honestly never thought he could balance a relationship with just one woman and his career with as much as he was gone. Most of the men on his team, save Doc, never had any relationships that lasted very long. Two of the men on his team had tried marriage once, but they were already divorced, their marriages had lasted less than a year combined. But Joe didn't let that deter him.

For Joe, being in a relationship with any woman was new for him. He was a man who didn't do commitment. He preferred to fuck whatever willing pussy he could find, then walk away as soon as he nutted off, he didn't do the sentimental and emotional bullshit. He had no bloody time for that shit, or so he thought. When he met Laura, all his rules went out the window after bitch slapping him in the face on the way out. He fought against his feelings, telling himself he didn't have time or his career simply didn't allow himself to be with just one woman, even went as far as claiming he would miss his freedom. Then life gave him a very surreal kick in the ass that nearly tore his heart in two and now here they were, a blissful year later just as happy as ever. He had given up the apartment he had shared with his brother Marcus and their sister Katilen, moved in with Laura and Cody, her son from a previous marriage, loving every minute of it.

Despite his career having him gone days, weeks, months, or on occasion a year, he wouldn't change a thing. Their relationship required some sacrifice and trust because of both of their careers that put them in the line of fire, but they made it work. His family loved Laura and Cody just as if they were one of their own. Five of his brothers had already met her, joking with her all the time about dumping him to give them a chance, and she talked to his parents at least once a week. They have all told him (including the brothers and sisters back in the UK) that if he ever hurt her or Cody, they would disown him and keep her. He was so glad they accepted her after meeting her family, seeing how they treated her. After he'd shared her family past with his parents, he had to hold them back from coming here to confront her parents. What was even more special was that his family included her brother Dominick, who was also a police officer for San

Diego Police Department, in all the family festivities as well.

Joe squeezed her into him tighter as he leaned down putting his nose into Laura's neck to breathe in her scent while giving thanks to God above that she was still here with him. Laura leaned her head back into Joe's chest as she continued to turn over the bacon in the pan. He knew she cherished their mornings together when it was just the two of them before they had to face the evils of the world. Cody was already off to school, so that gave them some time to be adults and just relax with each other. Joe, like Laura, knew they were given a miracle when they were allowed evenings together without being rushed or running late into the night with whatever they had thrown their way. While she never said anything, Joe knew she hated the missions that kept him away for weeks at a time. He missed her like hell and could tell on the rare occasions that he could call home that she was trying hard not to cry from the joy of hearing his voice or ask a million questions, she knew she couldn't know where he was at and the calls sometimes didn't happen.

Moving away from Joe's arms, she scooped the eggs and bacon onto their plates and handed them to Joe while she placed the pans into the sink to soak before following him over to the table. As she got closer to the table, Joe grabbed her by the waist and pulled her into his lap, kissing her lips as she sat down.

"Hey when did you get home?"

"Late last night love. How was ye day yesterday? Ye were sound asleep, didn't even stir when I gave ye a kiss te let ye know I was home."

"It was hell yesterday. Did a late evening raid on a warehouse, Alpha Squad-5, bad guys-0."

Joe leaned over to nip her shoulder. "Aye lass, glad ye all made it out ok."

"Hey mister, food in your stomach, no play time," Laura laughed as Joe tickled her side.

"I can't keep my hands or mouth off of ye right now. I didn't get te see ye for two weeks and ye were plum out when I got home. I have a lot te make up for, love. I don't honestly think there would be a day I would nae want ye with every chance we have alone. Even when we are sixty, I'll be chasing ye beautiful arse around the bedroom."

"You do know that shit eventually wears off, right? Eventually you'll get tired of my face or start thinking of wanting a younger piece of ass."

Joe stood up with Laura in his arms and walked toward the bedroom pissed off. He threw her onto the bed, grabbing her ankles when she started to push away from him to get away. He flipped her on to her stomach and drew her over his lap pushing his shirt that she was wearing over her head and using it to tie her hands behind her back. Since she hadn't worn any underwear, that meant less work for him.

"What did ye just say, lass? How many times have we gone for this shite?" WHACK. "Did I nae say that shite was finished?" WHACK. "I have told ye and told ye, time and time again, there is nae other. There will nae be another. Ye are it for me." WHACK, WHACK, WHACK. Her ass was nice and red and Laura was screaming his name while fighting to get off his lap. The sight had his cock stiffening, begging for attention.

Joe stood up and dropped her face first into the mattress as he pushed his sweatpants down. He leaned down to position Laura just right, keeping her hands behind her back and dove face first into her dripping pussy. He licked, nibbled, and sucked her juices streaming out of her pink pussy as if he was starved. When he got his first taste of what he'd been craving for the last two weeks, he stood up and without warning or gentleness, rammed his steel rod cock into her pussy and pounded away. He wrapped her hair around one hand, using it to pull her back to him while holding her tied hands with the other to anchor himself.

"Does this cock feel like it will ever get enough of ye fucking cunt, love? This cock doesn't want another. I will fuck ye senseless until ye finally realize what I'm talking about. I told ye I claimed ye the first time I fucked ye love. Ye are it and eventually ye will realize I am nae ever leaving ye. Maybe if I bred ye a few times, ye will get the picture. What do ye think lass? Should I plant my seed in ye?" Joe punctuated each statement with a harsh thrust.

Joe knew Laura lost her control when he dominated her. He knew what buttons to push and when. She had shared how much she loved it when he took total control, especially in the bedroom. When he talked about breeding her, her body's response was visceral. Though they hadn't talked about a baby before, the idea of giving her his child turned him on to a new level.

In her excitement, Laura changed up her hip thrusts to take him deeper. He rewarded her with a smack on the ass. Joe grabbed her hair tighter and pulled her literally back against him, taking his hand off the shirt at her wrists and placing it on her throat.

"Nae lass, I'm in control of this ride. I didn't say you can come or enjoy this. I think ye body liked the idea of me breeding ye. I'm going te fuck ye nice and hard love. I'm going te feed it my seed and pray it takes. It would be nice to have a wee babe running around with ye eyes and hair. A little lass or a little mannie that Cody can play with. Aye, I think that's what I am going te do, lass."

Joe guided Laura back down onto the mattress grabbing her hips with both hands and hammered her pussy. Pulling out, he ran his fingers around her clit and through her folds, spreading her juices toward her back hole. He chuckled as she tensed just a tiny bit. Sinking his hard cock back into her pussy balls deep, rotating his hips as he hit her womb, he slid his thumb into her puckered hole and started a tempo that drove her over that edge fast and hard. Joe felt a tingle crawl slowly up his spine letting him know it's going to be a long and hard orgasm for him. Gripping her hip tighter, he pulled her back into him harder.

"Aye lass, this is going te be good. I want te feel ye pussy gripping my cock hard love. Fuck I love ye pussy sucking my cock dry. Give it te me. Come for me."

Joe grabbed a tight hold onto her hair, pulling

her head back toward him devouring her lips just has he felt her control snap, drenching his cock in her juices. Three thrusts later, he was covering her walls with his cum as he slammed one last time into her tight pussy. Holding her tightly against him, he rolled his hips to get deeper, wishing he could bury himself inside her and never leave. Untying her hands, he slowly withdrew from her warmth and pulled them both into the bed, covering them up, pulling her in his arms, falling asleep blissfully. Both were too drained to move any further to get cleaned up. Joe loved being able to hold Laura in his arms and fall asleep. To him this was heaven.

———

LAURA WOKE with a start then realized it was the phone that had roused her from sleep. Reaching over Joe, she picked up her cell phone that was laying on the nightstand next to the bed. "Pratt."

"Where the hell are you? Thought you were meeting me at the gym," Raso demanded.

"Sorry something came up. What's going on?"

"I'm sure something came up alright, let me guess the Scottish studmuffin came home from his travels to outer space?"

"Moving on, what's up?"

"We just got called in for a case. Apparently it was Team Two, Charlie Squad's turn to take a new case, but the family of one of the girls happens to know someone in the top brass. Alpha Squad is getting the call instead because they want the best. Get untangled from squidward and get the booty moving sister," Raso informed Laura.

"You know if he hears you calling him squidward, payback is going to be a bitch, right?"

"He won't hear unless you tell him."

"Aye lass, I just heard it myself, so that means the payback is going te be sweet Raso," Joe said into the phone at Laura's ear.

Raso squeaked, "Oh shit, Hi Highlander Sorry, I didn't know you were there."

Joe laughed. "I'm sure ye didn't, lass. I'll try nae to be evil in my plot against ye. How are ye doing today?"

"Trying to keep me from getting your girl out of the bed mister? Sorry Charlie, but we just got a case and boss lady wants her tushie in the conference room with the rest of us."

"Aye and such a fine tushie she has. I will get her te ye pronto." Joe laughed caressing Laura's ass.

Laura snickered at the exchange between Joe and

Raso. He loved to mess with her and the others on the team. He made jokes with them about members of Alpha Squad and his SEAL team hooking up to "keep it in the teams". She got up and went to put her uniform on to head into HQ. She had a feeling it was going to be a long day if Alpha Squad was being requested for this assignment. That was never a good thing despite them being the best in the department. After putting on her duty belt, she leaned over toward Joe and gave him a quick kiss.

"I'll call and let you know how things are looking. Are you good for getting Cody from school if I have to work past his pick-up time?"

"Aye lass, I got the little mannie today. I promised him we'd work on his batting and mitt since he wants te play little league this summer. Go on with ye, get te work so that ye can get home faster. I love ye, lass." Joe kissed Laura as he got up from the bed and walked toward the shower, winking at her when he caught her staring at his ass.

2

Laura walked into the Alpha Squad Conference room and smacked Raso on the back of the head. "Hey, what the fuck Red?" Raso exclaimed in surprise.

"That's for messing with Highlander on the phone. You're lucky he was in a good mood with your cracks this morning, you goob."

"Yeah, yeah, if I didn't make his life a little hard when we talked then he would think I liked him."

"Keep dreaming, twatwaffle. I still say you should hook up with Mac instead of just being friends." Laura laughed.

Raso gagged, "Whatever, not into bestiality. That fool is too much of a dog for my taste. He's a great friend but that's it."

"What, our dear friend isn't admitting that she is hankering after her own Scottish studmuffin, the jarhead brother, Marcus," Diesel spilled as she walked into the room.

"Oh, really now? Is what Diesel just said true, my dear Raso? If it is, I can talk with Joe to set you two up." Laura wiggled her eyebrows at Raso while she laughed.

"Fuck you both. I would like a real man, not someone else's child, thank you very fucking much," Raso said as she flipped Laura and Diesel off.

"Awww Raso, everyone started out someone's child. Some just grow up better than others." Diesel walked away laughing.

Everyone busted out laughing at Raso, Laura, and Diesel's exchange, then moved on to discussing the newest Star Wars movie getting ready to come out. The teams always got together with some of the victims they rescued and kept in touch with them, taking them to the movies or doing something as a group to make them feel comfortable and safe in society again. They wanted to help them realize their potential when the rest of the world tended to forget them and let them become a statistic. This is partly why they were so successful. During their conversation about a possible camping trip, Captain Katherine Irby and Lt. Jessica Haile came in.

"Alright ladies, let's get this show on the road. Looks like four girls disappeared from the BlueMan arcade two nights ago and the parents were none the wiser due to the girls all claiming they were staying at the other's house. Only one of the four parents knew that the girls had gone there because the kid actually told her mom something. The victims are Tabitha Jennings age 15, Danika Starr age 16, Juanita Sanchez age 15, and Farzooh Nadinaez age 15. The arcade owner, Dennis Ackerman, told the responding officer for Seaside City PD that he saw the girls come in but then had gone into the back where his office is located. He says he never saw them leave or what happened to them after going into his office. He just assumed they went home. He does have cameras in the facility but states they are only for show to deter would be criminals from doing anything in the place so there are no recordings," Captain Irby informed Alpha Squad.

"Great, so not only is he useless as a manager but he's got fake equipment to make it look like he's a good guy. So what's our plan with this one? The parents are pushing for us to check into this guy, right?" Rameriez asked.

"That's pretty much our take too, Rameriez. The plan of action is to pair you guys up and have each of you to talk with the parents separately. I also want one of to talk with the arcade manager and give me your take. Pratt, I want you and Cortez to pair up, talk with Tabitha Jennings' parents. The parents, Richard and Diane Jennings, are divorced and like to bicker back and forth from my understanding. You two are good at dealing with parents like that. When you're done with them, I want you two to also take the arcade owner since you two have a good bullshit meter with people like this," Irby looked down at her paper as she walked over toward Raso.

"Raso, you're with York. You two talk with Marita Sanchez. She's a single mom since the father passed away approximately six years ago in Iraq. Raso, you're a single mom so I think you'll be able to identify with her since I have Pratt working with Cortez on the Jennings and the arcade manager." Irby smiled at Raso as she made eye contact before moving over to Rameriez and Diesel.

"Rameriez, I put you with Diesel on this one, and I want you two to talk to Mohummad and Nazirina Nadinaez. Apparently it was their daughter who told the mother where they were going so we have a starting point." Irby nodded to them before making eye contact with her second-in-command.

"Lt. Haile, I'm putting you back in the field and teaming you up with Sgt. Brocard for this case. You two are going to go and talk with Dr. Abel and his wife, Karen Starr. These two are wealthy and holier than thou. They like to think they are running this show because he's a doctor and they have money. You two know as well as I do if I put either one of these other six detectives on them, we'll have issues because our girls don't take shit from people and these two think we are beneath them, lower than-pond-scum. I don't play that game and neither will you two. I want you two to make it very clear our detectives will run this show, so you two have permission to put them in their place as you see fit," Captain Irby informed her two ranking officers before turning to look at each Detective in the conference room. After looking at each one and nodding, Captain Irby walked out of the room.

"Oh goodie, we get the arcade and the bitter-snatch parents. Pratt, how the hell did we wind up the bullshit meter maids? I thought that was Diesel and Raso," Cortez quipped.

"Well Raso has a good b.s. meter too, but Diesel would probably knock their heads off their shoulders. I think we've knocked one too many heads together as well, but who knows. Let's get this adventure dealt with so I can get home at a decent hour and enjoy sloppy joe night with the boys," Laura said.

"Awww, already calling him sloppy Joe? Thought SEALs were supposed to be clean freaks?" Diesel laughed.

Laura walked over and smacked Diesel on the back of the head. "It's food, you moron. If you actually cooked instead of eating out all the time or stopped dating pussy boys then you'd know what we were talking about. Jeezus."

The team had a few more laughs before going to their vehicles. Laura and Cortez headed to their SUV and pondered which interview to tackle first. "Do we want to get the sleezeball over with first or do we want to talk with the parents to get a better idea of what to watch for with said sleezeball?"

"Let's hit the parents first, Taz. If they are divorced, more than likely they are at each other's throats. Let's go put them out of each other's misery so they can go their separate ways without causing bloodshed. They already know someone is coming by to talk to them. I'm not sure why we have the case yet since it's not for sure they are human trafficking victims, but better safe than sorry."

Detectives Laura 'Red' Pratt and Tarilyn 'Taz' Cortez drove to the home of Diane Jennings. The mother and the father were waiting there to speak with the detectives taking over the case and see where they were at in the investigation. Both women knew the drill with parents in the beginning of any investigation. The parents blamed themselves and each other, especially if there was any animosity between them. They saw it time and time again during investigations.

Laura and Cortez arrived at the mother's house and knocked on the door. A woman in her late thirties opened the door with red eyes, hair in a messy bun wearing sweat pants, and a baggy t-shirt. "Hello, I'm Detective Pratt and this is Detective Cortez. Are you Ms. Jennings?"

"Oh yes, I'm Diane. I'm sorry, please come in. I'm sorry I am a mess. My ex-husband is in the living room pacing. Please come in."

"No worries ma'am, we understand this is a very upsetting time. Just know that we are doing everything we can to find your daughter and her friends."

Laura and Cortez followed Diane into the house, into the living room, and stopped by the couches.

"Diane, who the hell was at the door? Don't walk away when I'm talking to you damn it," yelled a man standing in the living room.

Laura looked over at Diane who stood near the archway by the door. She was in her late thirties wearing no makeup with red eyes that revealed tiredness from lack of sleep but she was otherwise beautiful. She looked like she wanted to crawl into a deep dark corner and escape from the rest of the world, but most of all from the man in the living room. The exchange between Diane and her ex made Laura suspect that the husband was a jerk who belittled the ex-wife on a daily basis and possibly more so since the daughter went missing. Only time would tell during this interview.

"Excuse you sir, I'm Detective Cortez and this is Detective Pratt with the Riverton County Sheriff's Department. We are the reason she walked away from you, so she could answer the door. We are here investigating the disappearance of your daughter and her friends."

"It's about damn time someone showed up to talk with us. This is bullshit. I knew I should have gone for custody when we went through our divorce. I knew her fucking ass couldn't take care of my daughter and I should have followed my gut. She's just as useless now as when we were married," Richard Jennings yelled at Laura and Cortez.

"Richard, I thought she was at a friend's house. We were the same way when we were kids. You can't blame this on me," Diane stated quietly.

"Yes I can because you should have called that brat's parents and made sure it was the truth. Now because of you, our daughter is missing."

"Mr. Jennings, I'm sorry but we will not tolerate you bashing your wife over your daughter's disappearance. Kids will be kids, and sometimes these things happen. It doesn't mean it's your wife's fault. In case you're forgetting, there are three other girls missing along with your daughter, so stop blaming your ex-wife," Cortez reminding Richard Jennings in a firm tone.

He simply laughed. "Just like a fucking woman taking sides. IF she had done what a real mother did, hell if any of them had done what a real mother should, we wouldn't be going through this right now."

"Mr. Jennings, one of the girls did tell their mother where they were going. They were all planning on staying at one of the girl's home. Those parents thought they were at a friend's house helping her pack for the same sleep over they assumed their kid was going to. So if anyone is to be blamed, it's the kids for lying to their parents, not the parents. Now when you're ready to talk like an adult and not act like a child, then we can get down to business," Laura stated.

"It's ok, Detectives. Richard is just upset our daughter is missing. No harm. How can we help you find our daughter?" Diane quietly stated.

"Well, we do have several questions in regards to your daughter. Do you know if she's been to this arcade before?" Laura asked.

"Yes ma'am, she has. She and her friends like to go there to play some dance arcade game there where you can step on it and try to remember the colors or something with a big screen tv on it. They liked to play on it, saying it helped them with their cheerleading practice. They were planning to try out for the cheerleading squad."

"Yeah like that's going to happen with her ass as big as it is. I told you that you needed to curb her fucking eating habits," Richard sneered.

"Mr. Jennings, this is the last time you're being warned. If there's so much as one more rude outburst and you can continue this discussion down at the station. Your daughter is missing and that's my concern right now, not your bullshit attitude about how her mother sees fit to parent. Now sit down and shut the hell up," Laura ordered.

Cortez reached over and patted Laura's arm as she leaned over, "Hey it's ok, don't let his assiness get to you, chica."

After an hour of talking with the Jennings, the two headed over to the BlueMan Arcade to speak with the manager. When they arrived, there were kids going in and out of the establishment. "Shouldn't these heathens be in school right now? I mean come on, it's the middle of the day."

Laura laughed at Cortez's assessment of the kids. "Taz, they are on spring break. They are out for at least a week right now so no there is no school."

"Wasn't that last week? I mean seriously shouldn't these things be learning how to take over the world and make our lives miserable and all? Don't get me wrong, I love little Cody but these brats, just ugh," Cortez complained, staring at the kids through the car windshield.

Laura shook her head. "Spring break varies from school-to-school or district-to-district. Cody was out last week while these kids get out this week. Just wait until you have yours."

"Oh hell to the no, this chick ain't having any of

that Kool aide. Nope, not happening captain." Cortez shook her head.

Both women laughed as they got out of the car and headed into the arcade that was overflowing with the kids coming and going. When they walked into the building, they requested to speak with Dennis Ackerman. The kid behind the counter picked up his phone and called the manager. When the worker hung up, he stated that the manager would be out in a few minutes. Taking advantage of that time, Laura and Cortez looked around at the surroundings trying to get an idea of what the girls saw and went through when they disappeared.

"You know they may not have been taken from here. If they walked or took the bus then they could have been taken along the way," Cortez stated as she looked around.

"True, but here's my issue, how do we know which house they left from? We need to get everyone back together and look at time lines for these kids. I highly doubt we're going to get a decent time line from this guy by the looks of this place," Laura commented.

The owner for the BlueMan Arcade came up to them and introduced himself. "Hello, I'm Dennis

Ackerman. I'm the owner of this establishment. How may I help you?"

"Hello I'm Detective Pratt and this is Detective Cortez. We are investigating the disappearance of four missing girls. They were last seen at this arcade, and we are trying to find out anything we can about their disappearance. I know you spoke with an officer from Seaside City PD already, but we have taken over this investigation at the request of the parents. We have a few questions for you if you have a few moments."

"Oh yeah," Dennis Ackerman responds hesitantly. "Ok sure, what can I do for you?"

"You told the previous officer that you saw the girls come in but you left to go to your office in the back, is that correct?" Cortez asked.

"Yes, that's correct. I saw them come in and go over to the video game area over there," Ackerman pointed to the back area furthest from the door. Laura and Cortez looked to their right which had their back to the door. "They all separated at first so I didn't think anything of it," Ackerman continued.

"Ok, do you know how long they stayed?" Laura questioned.

Ackerman shuffled around a little, sliding his hands into his pants pockets, refusing to look into their eyes yet getting upset with the questions. "No I don't, I'm sorry. As I said before, I went into my office to do some paperwork and get caught up with some stuff since I had been out last week due to a family member's death. Is there anything else?"

"We still have questions. You told the officer your cameras are for deterring theft. What kinds of theft have you been dealing with?" Cortez asked, purposely keeping him from going to the back.

"Well, we haven't had any per say, which is why I said they are there to deter it. They aren't operational, but no one knows that yet. I like to think that is what keeps them from doing anything," Ackerman answered stiffly.

Cortez stared at Ackerman for several seconds then shrugged. "Ok thank you, that's all for now. We'll be in touch."

Laura and Cortez left looking at each other as they walked out. They both didn't like the answers they received from the manager for some reason. When they got into the SUV, Cortez took her phone out. "I think we need to have this guy looked into. My b.s. meter was going off the Richter scale on this guy."

"Yeah, mine too. Let's head back to HQ and debrief then go from there. Joe should be picking up

Cody in a few minutes, so not sure what the man is cooking but I'd like to spend a little bit of time with him before we dive deep into this one."

Laura and Cortez headed back to the HQ conference room to meet up with the others on Alpha Squad. For the next two hours, they went over notes and comments from the parents and the arcade manager, discussing time lines and their next step in the investigation. They all agreed that something didn't add up with this case.

"On the outside, this guy looks clean and so do all the parents, but we need more background on them. Something just doesn't ring right with this whole thing. We've done this long enough to know when something isn't on the up and up with the statements. I want to make sure these parents aren't in dire straits to the point they would consider selling their kids and their friends or whatever the case may be. Pratt, you said the guy who owns the arcade gave you the creeps?" Captain Irby questioned after heavy discussions.

"Wasn't just me Captain, even Cortez said she'd rather face those clown freaks stepping out of the woods near her place than deal with this guy. I agree, I'd rather deal with the clowns since I can shoot their asses and get away with it on the self-defense rule. This guy just weirds us out and it's illegal to shoot someone for being weird."

Captain Irby nodded after thinking for a few seconds. "Ok, I'm calling our computer expert and seeing what we can find out. Go home and get some rest. I want everyone back in here at 0700 hours ready to tackle this head on. Hopefully we can find some more information."

3

––––––––––

Everyone headed out after the meeting ended. Laura called Joe to see if she needed to pick up Cody or if he'd already gotten him, but got her answer when Cody picked up. What she didn't expect was to hear a woman speaking in the background. She felt jealous but since she didn't know where they were, she couldn't really react so she headed home to wait for them.

"Laura, are ye home?" Joe yelled out as he and Cody walked into the house.

"Yep, I'm in the kitchen. How was your day? Hey Cody, get started on homework. I'm making your snack for you."

"That's ok mom, Joe took me for ice cream. That's where we were when you called." Cody hugged Laura before running to his room to do his homework.

"Oh, ok." Laura walked out of the kitchen and headed to the bedroom to get out of her uniform.

"Lass, what's wrong? Ye seem upset," Joe asked following Laura into the bedroom.

"I'm good, Joe. Just a lot on my mind with this case that's all."

"Uh huh, nice try love. Talk te me. I can see that look on ye face like ye feel hurt or something. Are you upset I took little mannie te the ice cream place with Wolf, his team, and their families?"

"Who was the girl you were talking to in the background?" Laura blurted.

"Ah, so ye think I was messing around on ye with Cody around, is that it? Laura, that was Caroline I was talking te, wanting te know if I was coming te the cookout that she is having in a couple of weeks for Wolf's SEAL team and mine. She wants ye and Cody te come as well. I was telling her ye would be there if I have te drag ye there with me. They are good women and would love te meet ye." Joe reached over pulling Laura into his arms. "Laura, I have been with ye, in ye, and loving ye for a year now. I am nae going te wander from ye. Ye can ask the men on my team and ye can ask Wolf, as well as his team members the same question - there is nae one else for me. Ye are it and I will tell ye until I am blue in the face, I love ye, lass."

"I love you too, Joe. I'm sorry. I keep waiting for you to look at me and say it's over and that you decided you want someone who is better," Laura mumbled into Joe's chest.

"Och lass, ye are the only woman for me," Joe leaned down and kissed her on the lips gently. "Ye are lucky Cody is still awake or I'd be tanning this delicious ass of ye right now. Ye will be punished later when he's in bed. So don't think ye got away with it, love."

Laura looked up at Joe shyly looking at him through her lashes, "Yes sir." She stood up on tippy toes, kissing his lips quickly and then made her escape down the hall to the bathroom to grab a quick shower.

During dinner they talked about their day, what they could talk of, with laughter and jokes between the three of them. Joe teased Cody about a girl in his class that he didn't like. After dinner was done, they cleaned the kitchen then retired to the living room to watch a show together as a family, curled up on the sofa. Joe sat at one end with Cody in the middle, for now. Joe had his arm across the back of the couch making sure he was touching Laura's shoulder or her hair. At bedtime they tucked Cody into his bed, reading to him his nightly story before retiring to their bedroom.

———

As soon as they stepped into their bedroom, Joe followed through with his earlier promise. "Take ye clothes off lass and stand by the end of the bed *now*."

Laura quickly disrobed, knowing she had upset him with her earlier statements and that her punishment was going to be doled out. Joe disrobed down to his boxers when he saw Laura standing near the end of the bed and walked up behind her pulling her body into his, her back to his front, his hand going into her hair, yanking her head to the side, his mouth leaving a hot trail going down her neck. He could feel her pulse beating away beneath his lips, it felt like a horse galloping away. He couldn't tell if she was scared or excited.

"It's obvious the spanking ye received this morning didn't work so I'm going te punish ye a different way love. Get on the bed and bend over. I want ye knees on the mattress and ye face te the side. Then place ye hands at ye ankle and don't move.

Arse in the air how I like it. Ye are nae allowed te come until I say that ye can. Do ye hear me?" Joe ordered in his low, hard voice at Laura's ear.

"That's not fair, damn it. I simply asked. Jesus. Ouch, that hurt."

Joe smacked Laura hard on her right ass cheek. "Aye love, it will hurt and ye didn't just ask who Caroline was, ye assumed I was cheating on ye with her. That's disrespectful te her, te Wolf, te me, and most of all, disrespectful te ye. Now hands at ye ankles and don't move until I tell ye te," Joe ordered.

Joe pulled out the Velcro cuffs he had in the drawer and cuffed Laura's right hand to her right ankle and her left hand to her left ankle, keeping her on her knees. He positioned her ass just the way he liked it while caressing her ass cheeks, then moved away from the bed, walking out of the room. He went into the kitchen to get a few things and then checked the locks on the windows, the front door, and then went and checked on Cody making sure he was still sleeping.

Taking his time to build up the anticipation, he stood in the doorway watching Laura squirm around on the bed. He finally decided enough was enough and wanted to feel her tight pussy squeezing his dick good so he went over to her and swatted her ass cheek. "Stop moving lass or I'll spank ye arse good and then take the back hole instead of ye pussy like I want. We have nae played this way before, but I will tonight te make ye understand I'm tired of ye putting yeself down or comparing yeself te other women. I don't want them, I want ye, and eventually ye will figure out I mean it."

Joe's index finger teased her puckered hole as he said words. They haven't tried anal play much, but he wouldn't be above doing it for punishment. Shaking his mind off of his thoughts, he moved his finger from her back hole down to her pussy and started circling her clit, teasing her just a little. Never touching the bud, just the outskirts. When Laura started moaning just a little, he stopped. Reaching over to the nightstand where he'd placed a large bowl, he got out an ice cube and lightly ran it over her puckered hole, chuckling at her gasp and attempt to get away. Joe swatted her ass telling her to settle down then moved the ice to her core, teasing the area and circling back up to her clit.

Deciding he wanted to taste her nipples as he teased her, Joe turned Laura over. Helping her onto her back, keeping her hands and ankles cuffed together, he rubbed a cube on one nipple getting it rock hard while he sucked and nibbled on the other one then switched nipples until the ice cube melted. Once that cube melted, he grabbed another one from the bowl and moved down to her clit, slowly dragging the ice cube over her bundle of nerves while he tongued her tight pussy, bringing her to a frenzy. When he felt her reach that edge, he backed away, stood up, and he put the cube in his mouth crunching on the ice staring at her. She had murder in her eyes because he withheld her orgasm, but that only made Joe chuckle just a little. He slowly took his boxers off, stroking his painfully hard cock as he held her gaze.

Grabbing another ice cube, he bent over to continue to lick, suck, and nip on her clit while he fucked her pussy with the ice cube, never giving her the full amount of the pleasure she sought. He could taste her frustration. He continued this sweet torture for an hour, driving her completely insane pleading with him to let her come until she had tears streaming down her face. Laura begged Joe for forgiveness, telling him she loved him and begging him to fuck her so she could come. Each time Joe backed away for a moment before going right back in and starting all over again.

Finally deciding that he needed his release just as much as she did, he leaned over her, staring into her eyes, one hand wrapped around her throat and the other steading himself on the bed, he slammed his hard cock into her dripping pussy as growled down at her. "Don't ye dare come lass. Nae until I tell ye te. If ye come I will pull out and come all over ye tits and go stay at my brother's place. Ye pissed me off thinking I would cheat on ye with Cody in tow. That makes me feel like ye don't trust me and that hurt, lass. I love ye so fucking much but I will nae tolerate such disrespect."

Joe rode Laura hard, never breaking eye contact as he slammed his cock into her over and over. Laura opened her mouth in a silent scream as she stared up at Joe. "Oh Joe, please let me come, please."

Joe rammed a few more times into her hard as he leaned down nipping the side of her lips at the same time he growled, "*Tha mi sa' ghaol leat Bidh gaol agam ort fad mo bheatha, thusa 's gun duine eile mo chridhe croie.* Fuck love come, fuck this is going to be an intense one."

He slammed into Laura one last time, growling her name as he came hard inciting her release, which had Laura lifting her head from the mattress and screaming Joe's name into his neck, shaking from head to toe. When she was able to recover her breath, Laura whispered, "I'm sorry, Oh God, I'm sorry, Joe. I love you."

When Joe could move, he kissed her forehead and reached down to undo the cuffs from her hand and ankles, then pulled Laura into his arms entangling their limbs together. In the year that they had been together, they had realized that they couldn't sleep very well without being wrapped around each other. Joe had never been able to sleep like that with any other women in his past. As soon as he hit it, he left, never looking back or at the woman again. Since being with Laura, he couldn't live without touching her in some way, asleep or awake. They usually woke up with him lying on top of her with limbs entwined or vice versa.

"Ok lass, what is on ye mind? Ye said this new case has ye troubled. Talk te me," Joe said into Laura's hair.

"Four girls went missing the yesterday. They had all lied to their parents telling them they were staying at one of the other friend's house so they could go to this arcade. Apparently they liked to go to this place called the BlueMan Arcade for some dancing game thing they have there because they wanted to practice for the cheerleading squad next year. Sometime between arriving there and leaving, they were kidnapped. So far no ransom demands have been made and nothing indicates that they ran away," Laura explained to Joe as she curled up to him a little more closely.

"OK, but that's normally where ye lasses come in. What's bothering ye about this case more than normal?"

"The dad of the girl we went to interview today - he was really harsh with his ex-wife. It made me feel like I was dealing with my ex-husband. Cortez had to put her hand on me to calm me down because I started to go off on the bastard. What made it worse was when we went into the arcade, the owner gave us really bad creepy vibes. We both feel like he's lying about the cameras in the place. I think he personally uses them to perv on the kids. I believe he knows more than he's saying. Captain is calling our computer expert back in from her vacation, which sucks, but we need her big time on this one. I hate to think what these girls are going through right now." Laura sighed as she kissed Joe's chest before laying her head back down.

"Aye love, I understand. Tell ye what, I can make a call te a friend of mine named Tex, who is way better at computers than any guys ye can get, he isn't going to have to deal with the red tape ye guys will.

Let me know what information ye have on the parents and the arcade owner. I'll give them te Tex when I call him in the morning. Now relax and get some rest while ye can, something tells me ye lasses are going to have ye hands full with this until it's solved."

"Thanks, Joe. I appreciate it. I love you." Laura kissed Joe then finally drifted off. Joe waited until she was sound asleep before moving out from under her. When he made it to the living room with his cell in hand, he dialed a number and waited for the person on the other line to answer.

"Better be good to be calling me this late," came the growl on the other end of the line.

"Aye Tex, it's MacLeod. Sorry te bother ye this late, but it's important."

"Oh hey, no problem. What's up, man? Don't tell me you have a stalker and need help to get rid of her?" Tex laughed.

Joe chuckled. "Nae, nothing like that. The lass I'm going te marry has caught a case that's making her and her teammates antsy. That's nae a good thing with this bunch. She stated they all felt like the manager of this arcade place is hiding something. They are calling their computer geek back in from vacation te have her dig inte the parents and the arcade owner. I ken ye can dig deeper without the bullshite red tape holding ye up. Do ye have the time?"

Tex whistled, "Wow, the heartthrob from the highlands of Scotland has fallen. Welcome to the club, brother. If she managed to snag you then she must be something special. Between your team and Wolf's, it was running joke who could bag the most women between missions before they met their women. You said she's working on a case? What does she do?"

Joe smiled big. "Aye, she's special Tex. She's everything, both her and her son, Cody. She's a detective for the Riverton County Sheriff's Department, working on a special ops task force. The team specializes in human trafficking, going after the arseholes on domestic soil like we do on foreign soil. Her team is great and were the ones who handled Russell's case last year."

"I remember that one, Wolf told me about it. Give me the information and I'll check into it. And Joe, keep an eye on her, what she does isn't easy. I still make regular calls to Fiona when she has one of her episodes if Cookie is gone."

"Aye, I agree. She won't admit it, but I know how hard it is for them. I've had te calmed her down on many a night when she's in the middle of a night-mare, or a crying episode from one of her cases. I can't imagine what she goes through when I'm nae home te hold her. These lasses are like pitbulls on a case and don't rest until they have their bad guys behind bars. Thanks man, I owe ye one. Say hi te ye lasses for me."

Joe sat there for a few minutes reflecting on his conversation with Tex. Granted what Fiona, Cookie's wife, had gone through when she was abducted, beaten, and raped after being kidnapped and brought south of the border was worlds away from what Laura and her team experienced. The fact that they had to see what these victims went through during the course of rescuing them was bad enough. He made a mental note to let Wolf and Cookie know a little more about Laura since all they really knew about her profession was that she was a cop. With Fiona's past, as well as their Commanding Officer's wife, Julie, he would probably need to give them a heads up to talk with the wives to make sure they would be okay with Laura at the cookout in case she got a call or something. He never really thought of any of that until his talk with Tex tonight. Joe got up and went back to the bedroom and watched Laura sleep. He didn't care what the others thought - if she couldn't be there, then he wouldn't be there either, despite the rest of his team going. Laura was his life now and he wasn't going to exclude her in anything he did just because of her job.

4

———

The next several days were hectic for Alpha Squad. Between dealing with the victims' parents, fighting to verify if the cameras were indeed fake, the owner refusing to call them back, and not being able to get much information out of the school about the girls' habits, the team felt like they were hitting brick walls at a hundred miles an hour. To make matters worse for Laura, Joe and his team left that morning for a new mission that his team was up for which had put her in a bad mood. Just before quitting time, Laura got the call she wasn't aware she was awaiting.

"Riverton County Sheriff's Office, how may I help you?" Laura answered.

"Hello, may I speak with Detective Laura Pratt, please?" responded an unfamiliar male voice.

"This is Detective Pratt, how may I help you?"

"Hi Detective, my name is Tex. Joe gave me a call the other day asking for help with information on the parents and an arcade owner in the case you're working on," Tex informed Laura.

"Oh ok, I didn't know that he had made the call. I appreciate the help. It's been nuts around here, we're chasing our damn tails with this one. Neither the parents nor the owner of the arcade are cooperating with us. I'm trying to keep my work partner from popping a cap in his ass right now."

"I can understand how that goes. Let me know if she caps his ass, I'll make sure the charges go away for her." Tex chuckled at Laura's groan.

"For the love of God, please do not tell her that or she'll do it just to get away with it. I will not allow you to make her a bigger monster than she already is. Please tell me you have some good news in all this jungle of bullshit we're dealing with, Mr. Tex," Laura begged.

"It's just Tex ma'am. Not sure about good news, but I do have some that might help. Seems two of the parents are heading for divorce and are fighting for custody of the kids. They haven't filed just yet, but I was able to find information that shows they are headed that way. The father is a complete ass and the basically wants money to play all day. Neither one really cares about the kids, it's about control. Joe told me about the parents you interviewed the other day, and I can tell you the father is a control freak with issues where women are concerned. I have found several complaints filed against him for domestic violence."

"I knew he was an asshole, thanks for confirming that. Were you able to find anything on the arcade owner? I have this gut feeling he's lying about the cameras. They had the red light showing, but he swore it was just for show," Laura stated.

"Joe said you were smart. To answer your question, yes, he was lying about the cameras being fake. I was able to pull up footage for the week of the girl's disappearance and the week after. He kept them all stored on his computer system in his office."

"Please don't tell me how you got it, just that you got it," Laura said.

"I can have all that I have found sent to your computer for you and your team to review. I have to say I'm impressed with RCSO for creating the task force. I admit I was clueless they had created this team but from what I've found, I'm definitely impressed. Thank you for what you and your team do," Tex complimented.

"Yeah, we pretty much stay under the radar. We don't like publicity or advertisement. Not even other co-workers truly know what we do. We prefer this for the safety and security of the victims we are able to rescue."

"I can understand that. I hope the information I sent you helps. If you need anything else, just get in touch and I'll be more than happy to help out anyway I can. I mean it, Detective, be safe out there."

"Thank you, Tex. I really appreciate it more than you know. I will definitely reach out if we need more help. Have a good night."

Laura hung up and sent Cortez a text letting her know she just got some information they would want to sift through for the case. Laura checked her emails and sure enough there was an email from Tex. How the hell he got her email, she didn't know, but she was grateful he was able to help them. This case, although pretty routine, something just felt really off. That's what bothered her the most.

Cortez and Laura poured over the information they received from Tex and watched all three videos that he found. It wasn't good. In the first video it showed the girls walking into the arcade for the first time three months ago playing a few games before finding the dancing video game that Diane Jennings told them about. They watched all four girls playing on the machine separately and then again two at a time to challenge each other. They were at the arcade for a couple of hours. The second video showed the girls going directly to the dancing game. In this video, it showed the owner going up to the girls and standing behind Danika Star a little too close talking to all of them. Video three showed the day that the girls went missing. They saw the girls entering the arcade, going as usual to the dancing game and then ten minutes later Dennis Ackerman going over to talk to the girls for several minutes then going toward the back. Several minutes later the girls went out the front door and that was the end of it.

Cortez pulled out her phone and called Captain Irby and Sgt. Brocard to let them know they found video footage from the cameras that the owner said didn't work. Twenty minutes later, the Captain, the Lt, the Sgt., and Sheriff Phillips walked in.

"Detective Pratt, where did you get the video feed if the cameras were fake?" Sheriff Phillips asked.

"An anonymous person, sir. Is there any way we can get a warrant to search the place since he's been less than forthcoming or do we have any other grounds to obtain one? I strongly believe he has something to do with their abduction," Laura said.

"We can't use this to get a warrant. We need more. I understand you guys feel he's lying, and yes we know this came to us, but his attorney will eat us alive over this. He'll walk and we lose any chance to find those girls in a timely fashion. We need to find another way. Go back to the arcade and talk to him some more. Go at him harder. If need be, take another detective or the Sgt. and let it spook him or whatever it takes. Have someone else watching him from the time you guys leave there in case he leaves or do it yourselves. Do whatever it takes, legally, so that his attorney can't get him walking," Sheriff Phillips ordered.

"Fine. Pratt, you and Cortez go back and talk to the arcade owner some more. Lean on him just a little. Make it seem like you know he's lying. Stalk the son of a bitch, whatever it takes to get this fucker to confess. I want his balls in a vice so tight his own mother can't suck them out of a straw for him," Captain Irby demanded.

"Holy shit, Cap's pissed," Diesel whispered.

"What was that, Diesel?" Captain Irby asked.

Diesel coughed. "Nothing captain, just clearing my throat, ma'am."

Cortez and Laura left HQ after making backup plans in case there were problems. Twenty-five minutes later, they arrived at the BlueMan Arcade. When they walked into the building, the kid looked up then went as fast as he could to the phones while watching their every move. Cortez smirked as she watched the kid tell whoever he was talking to that they were there. Laura sent a text to the team that was sitting at the back of the arcade to keep an eye out in case they had a runner.

Cortez leaned up against the counter popping her bubble gum. "We're here to see your boss. Want to let him know that Detectives Cortez and Pratt are back to see him?"

"Sorry detectives, but Mr. Ackerman is in meetings. This isn't his only place of business. He has many fingers in different fields."

"Wow Taz, the kid just spoke like a good little boy or is that a good little spaz? I'm sure your boss does dip his fingers into many fields, probably underage fields, too. So listen up dicklint, get back on that phone and you let your boss know that we are here and that he needs to have a new meeting or we get warrants to search and seize every fucking thing here, as well as his other businesses, too. You have exactly five minutes to give us the answer we are looking for before Detective Cortez here makes the call that will fuck your boss's life up in more ways than one. Tick tock kid, tick tock," Laura informed the visibly upset kid.

Cortez and Laura walked a bit away from the kid to see what he would do. They acted like they were in a conversation while Cortez made a quick call to Sgt. Brocard on the sly, who was in the alley way to make sure there were no runners. They were hoping the kid thought they were calling for the warrants since he picked up the phone and made a call. Two minutes later the kid came over to them and let them know that Mr. Ackerman would see them in a couple of minutes then walked away.

"Hear that, Sgt.? It seems like he's in the house after all. He'll get to us in a few minutes," Cortez said.

"I heard. Get back to me after you've talked to him. I want to know what was said. We're just down the street if you need us. Be careful in there, I don't trust this guy as far as we can throw him. He's already lied to us once. Do this by the book so he can't get off on a technicality," Brocard ordered.

"We will. Talk to you in a few." Cortez hung up

the phone then turned to Laura. "Even Brocard is feeling uneasy about this guy. How do you want to handle this?"

"Let's just talk to him. See if any 'guests' come out this way or if they sneak out the back way. Brocard and York are just down the street and can see who pulls out the back way if they decide to go out that way."

Cortez and Laura heard a door opening and turned toward where Ackerman came through a door and headed toward them. "Detectives, this is becoming tiresome. I've already spoken with you and gave you everything that I have and told you what I know. Now what is so important that you have to interrupt an important business meeting?"

"Important business meeting, Mr. Ackerman? How is running an arcade important? Ordering more video games? Setting up proper maintenance for your video cameras that supposedly aren't working? Figuring out new ways to lie to the police about victims having actually been in here and you actually leading said victims to the back off the side where the cameras can't reach? Or are you brokering for their sales to the highest bidder? What can a low-life arcade owner have that's so important to merit doing 'business with someone?" pushed Cortez.

Ackerman growled deep into his throat. "Detective, I'm not sure what your game is, but this is harassment and I do not and will not speak to you anymore. If you have anything further to say to me, please contact my attorney."

"That's ok, we already have more than enough information needed to go after you. So have a nice day. I'll be sure to forward your attorney a copy of the video we have from the same camera you claimed was broken. It was actually sent to us by an anonymous Good Samaritan to show that you were lying about the camera. Don't leave town, Mr. Ackerman. Toodles." Laura smiled, as she and Cortez turned and walked away.

"He's up to something. Twenty bucks says he's meeting someone to offload those kids and get them out of here as soon as possible. We need to have someone watching this place while we do some more digging on this SOB," Cortez stated as she turned back around to take one last look at Ackerman. She saw that he was watching them leave the building with a dark look in his eyes.

As they left the arcade, they made the call to Sgt. Brocard with their thoughts and agreed the team was to meet up somewhere for lunch to discuss their options and to talk with the captain about having patrol watch the area make sure no one left with the girls if they were being held there.

52

5
_____

For the next couple of days, Laura and Cortez ran down leads of all sightings of the girls from the time they left their homes, from the fast food restaurant they were seen in having lunch, the library they had told their parents they were going to do some studying, and to the park it was believed they were believed to be seen at one time before going to the arcade. It was even stated by one passerby they could have been there after the arcade but it was highly doubtful.

After they left the arcade a few days prior, Ackerman had gone underground and he hadn't been seen or heard from since their confrontation about the video camera. Laura sent an email to Tex, asking him if he could keep an eye on the camera to make sure he wasn't sneaking in when the patrols weren't catching him. Laura knew Tex would help them find anything on the girls they could use on possible locations they could be held. Laura sent a silent thank you every day for Joe sending Tex her way. She just prayed they could come up with where the girls were before it was too late.

Across the room, a phone rang.

"Cortez."

After a short pause, Laura heard Taz exclaim, "A body? Shit, who is it? Hold on, let me put you on speaker and have you speak to my partner, too. We're working a case at BlueMan Arcade. She might have an idea."

Laura heard Cortez yell out for her, "Yo, Pratt, come here. We got a call from Officer Brooklyn with San Diego PD about a body found outside the arcade."

Putting the officer on speaker, Cortez said, "Officer Brooklyn, I have you on speaker. Detective Pratt is here with me. You said my card was found on a body in the alley near BlueMan Arcade?"

"Yes ma'am, it was found in his back pocket stuffed into his wallet. According to the ID found on the body, kid's name is Timothy Masters. Do you know who he is?" Officer Brooklyn responded.

Cortez went through her notes on the case to see if the name shows up. "Sorry, no his name doesn't sound familiar."

"Officer Brooklyn, is there any way you can send me a pic from your phone to show me what he looks like?" Cortez rattled off her cell phone number off to Officer Brooklyn.

Right then, Cortez's phone pinged with an incoming text message. Laura picked up the phone while Cortez spoke with the officer on the phone. "Oh shit Taz, it's the kid behind the counter both times we went into the arcade."

Cortez put her head into her hand and mumbled a few choice words. "Yeah, it turns out we do know who it is, Officer Brooklyn. My partner and I will be there in about fifteen minutes to check out the scene. Has anyone checked the BlueMan Arcade for Dennis Ackerman? Masters worked at the arcade and Ackerman is under investigation for the disappearance for four girls."

"Yes ma'am, no one is responding when we knock on the door," came the officer's response.

"Why would you be knocking on the doors? Aren't they opened? It's after noon so they should be opened and packed with kids by now," Cortez said in a confused voice.

Officer Brooklyn sighed. "Well there was a line at the door. A couple of the kids said they had been waiting for them to open the doors. When we tried the doors, they were definitely locked. One of the kids said that the doors usually open around ten am, but no one responded when we knocked. We tried to call the owner, but there was no response on the number that shows for him."

"Shit, I bet you he's rabbited. Ok, thank you. We will be there in a few minutes." Cortez hung up the phone and looked at Laura. "I don't have a good feeling about this. Ackerman isn't at the arcade, the doors are locked, and the kid behind the counter is dead. I bet you Ackerman panicked about the video feed we mentioned. Damn it, he probably thought the kid gave it to us."

"Let's go tell Brocard the update and head out to the scene to see what we can find out. If that asshole is rabbiting then he's probably tying up loose ends." Laura grabbed her gun from her desk and holstered it while Cortez did the same thing.

Cortez and Laura went in search of Sgt. Brocard who was talking in the hall with Lt. Haile. "Hey guys. We just got a call from an Officer Brooklyn from San Diego PD. Apparently there was a body found in the alley behind the BlueMan Arcade."

"Why the hell were they calling you then?" Lt. Haile started to get pissed thinking someone was messing with her officers.

"Apparently the body is a Timothy Masters, the kid who worked behind the counter at the arcade. They got the call when some kid trying to find out why the arcade wasn't opened walked down the alleyway to see if there was another way in."

"Damn it, Cortez, I don't like this. What about Ackerman? Did they talk to him?" questioned Brocard.

"That's just it - the doors to the arcade are locked. No answer coming from inside the arcade nor is Ackerman answering his personal phone according to Officer Brooklyn," Cortez reported.

"Ok, you and Pratt go and check it out. But be careful," Haile told them.

Brocard nodded, agreeing with the Lt. "York and I will be about ten minutes behind you. Stay near the others. I'm with you guys on this. Something doesn't sound right with this scenario."

Arriving on scene, they saw Officer Brooklyn with another officer standing with him writing down notes while looking down at the body. He looked up and waived at both women. Cortez and Laura started to walk toward them. Cortez gave Laura a questioning side glance and then looked back at the two officers.

"You must be Officer Brooklyn, I am Detective Pratt and this is Detective Cortez, you spoke with us on the phone a little while ago. Officer, where is the crime scene team and medical examiner?"

Officer Brooklyn swayed from foot to foot slightly. "Sorry Detectives, we were ordered to call you and have your department handle it. We were just waiting for you to get here so you can call your crime scene and medical examiner."

"Officer, how long have you been on the job?" bristled Laura.

Officer Brooklyn started to respond when the officer with him spoke up, "Detective, I'm Officer Jenkins. I'm Officer Brooklyn's FTO. He's still train-ing. Like he said, we were ordered by our Sgt. to wait for you to arrive and hand the scene over to you. We questioned the orders just like you are, but that's our orders from our shift command. We can wait with you and help with the investigation to help give more information while we all wait for your crime scene techs and medical examiner to arrive."

Cortez and Laura stepped away from the group and placed a call to Sgt. Brocard so they could get the crime scene techs and a medical examiner rolling. As they turned around, a shot rang out of nowhere. Laura looked over to see Officer Jenkins fly back against the brick wall going down motionless. Officer Brooklyn, Laura, and Cortez drew their weapons while looking up for a shooter.

Suddenly, Brooklyn took off down the alley way, Laura and Cortez yelled for him to stop. They followed behind him to back him up when another shot rang out and Brooklyn went down with a hole between his eyes.

"Damn it, where the fuck is that shooter? It came from two different directions," whispered Cortez.

"Shit, what if we are surrounded? That means Brocard and York are going to be walking into an ambush along with our crime scene techs. We need to call and warn them." Pratt pulled out her phone and dialed York's phone to warn them what they would be pulling up into.

Just as York answered, the two heard a loud bang sounding further down the alleyway that had Laura and Cortez run toward it in hopes of catching the shooter. Laura grabbed her radio and informed dispatch shots were fired in the alleyway behind the BlueMan Arcade and two San Diego PD officers were down. Laura and Cortez could feel the hair on the back of their necks prickling.

Laura looked over at Cortez. "Something doesn't feel right about any of this. My gut is screaming. I think the asshole is playing with us. Why only shoot the two patrol officers and not us?"

Cortez looked at Laura nodding. "I think he's smarter than we gave him credit for. Me personally, I think he likes to play stupid to throw everyone off."

"Yeah, I'm starting to get that feeling, too. We were too loose with this case."

Cortez agreed with Laura's assessment of how they handled this case. "What the hell was that?" Cortez said, when a loud thunk sounded.

Both women turned around looking for origin of the noise. They slowly inched their way toward where they heard the sound. Hyper aware of everything around them and each other, they slowly moved forward until they heard a loud scream, not realizing it was their own screams as they were attacked from behind.

Both women went down, Cortez knocked out completely. Dennis Ackerman stepped over Cortez's body, kicking her in the process to make sure she was out. "Take both these bitches into the van. Mendoza is expecting them at the drop off site along with the other merchandise. If they wake up, knock them the hell back out. Do not let them escape or I'll let Mendoza have your carcass to do with as he pleases and I guarantee you won't like what he has in mind."

Ackerman looked from the two men that he gave the orders to down to the bodies of Laura and Cortez that they left lying in the dirty alley way, seeing that Laura was staring at him. "You bitches aren't so high and mighty now are you, you dumb bitch? Mendoza is going to have a blast breaking the both of you in. You have no idea who you've pissed off. It'll be interesting to see if he decides to just kill you or break you both then sell you. No one will ever find you two ever again." Ackerman stood up and walked away laughing when Laura finally gave in to the darkness.

Neither woman heard their Sgt. and teammate yelling their names over the phone trying to get them to respond. Neither woman nor kidnappers realized every word was heard as they walked away. Neither woman heard the small cries as they were loaded into the van. Neither woman felt the bumps and turns as they were driven from the alleyway toward their destination. Neither woman heard the calls go out on the radio trying to locate them. They just vanished into the wind.

6
____

Laura slowly came to as she heard her name being whispered loudly. Slowly opening her eyes, she realized the person saying her name was Cortez trying to make sure she was ok and their captors hadn't caused more harm than originally thought. Laura looked over at Cortez with questions in her eyes but unable to voice them because her throat hurt feeling like sandpaper sliding across skin.

"Hey beautiful, glad to see your eyes again," Cortez said.

Laura licked her very chapped lips. "Where are we? What the hell happened? Last thing I remembered was hearing a noise, turned around, and then nothing."

"Not sure exactly where we are, but we are being

held somewhere. I just woke up a few minutes ago. Not sure who took us but wouldn't be surprised if it was needlenose," Cortez started coughing as her throat became scratchy.

Suddenly the door opened and in walked a man that neither Cortez nor Laura knew. "Ola ladies. I'm glad to see that you beautiful senoritas have not suffered any serious damage in your trip to my humble abode. Well at least not any serious damage as of yet."

"Who the fuck are you and where are we?" Laura spat out as she tried to sit up as best as she could with her hands and feet tied.

"Ah you must be the spitfire one. The red hair kind of gives that away, senorita." The man clapped his hands with a huge smile. "To answer your questions my dear, my name is Francisco Mendoza, but you can call me Frank. I'm the son of a bitch you two whores have been looking for. Harassing my middle man on the whereabouts of my property tends to piss me off a little bit. The fact that you've been going in and out of his place of business tends to make people twitchy, and frankly, it's been interfering in my fucking business causing a ruckus. That tends to piss me off, so now you're dealing with me personally."

"Actually asshole, those girls are not your property just because they were dumb enough to walk into Ackerman's arcade. That's kidnapping. Look it up." Laura looked Mendoza straight in the eyes.

Mendoza backhanded Laura hard across the face. "Let me explain something to you putas. That establishment is mine. They came into it, making them my property while they are in there. It's not my problem their parents weren't responsible enough parents by letting them go somewhere alone. I take what I want, when I want. You bitches aren't in Kansas anymore. You're in my territory so what I say goes. And frankly my lovely bitches, I'm going to enjoy breaking the hell out of you."

Mendoza turned to his man at the door. "Bring the dark-haired bitch to the room. I think I'm going to start with her. Maybe if this cunt hears her friend screaming then she'll lose her attitude."

Mendoza walked out of the room leaving his man to go and grab Cortez. Laura fought against her binds to get to the man and stop him from dragging Cortez out of the room. The thug kicked Laura hard in the side knocking her over, then kicked her again in the head and laughed as he dragged a struggling Cortez out of the room. Laura heard whimpers coming from the other side of the room and looked.

She saw the four girls they had been searching for in the same room.

"Are you girls ok? Have they hurt you?" Laura asked the girls.

"We're ok for now. They haven't done anything other than keep us doped. Are you a cop? I'm Danika. I've been trying to keep these guys calm so those men don't get angry or anything."

"You're fine, Danika. It's best to keep calm and not give them what they want no matter what. They haven't touched you yet, have they?" Laura started to worry they were too late.

"No ma'am, they haven't raped us yet. I was scared that one of their men would have the way he was acting, but Mr. Ackerman was adamant to the guard that we were to be untouched. Although I don't know how long that's going to last now that we are here." Danika worried her lower lip.

Several hours later, the same thug, now jacketless, sweating, and his sleeves rolled up, brought in a motionless Cortez and dropped her onto the floor near Laura with a smirk. "Enjoy your freedom because your time under my fists is coming soon," he boasted in broken English.

When he left, Laura and Danika crawled over as best as they could to Cortez and checked on her. She was still breathing which made Laura relax just a little. "Taz, omg what did they do to you?"

"Ah, nothing really? They tried to get me to cry out or say who we spoke with about the case. They wanted names and I told him to bite my ass. You know the usual smartass shit we say and do. They hit like little bitches to be honest," croaked Cortez.

"Doesn't look like they hit like bitches," piped up Danika.

"Hey kid you're 16, watch the language. Your mother will have your ass and ours if you go home cursing like a sailor," Laura warned.

"Yeah like we're going to get out of here. You guys are cops. Not like they are going to come to Mexico or wherever we are to save us. We're not exactly in Kansas anymore, Dorothy. While you two sleeping beauties were knocked out the four of us weren't," came Danika's cheeky reply.

"Yeah well, they don't know about our connections and I guarantee when a particular Alpha male who has Pratt in his grasp can't be found, not even the hounds of hell will stop his ass from finding us. And let's not forget her brother when she's late picking up Cody," Cortez replied sounding hopeful.

"Don't hold your breath, Taz. He's deployed right now. I haven't spoken to him in a couple of days since he deployed other than when he was in air to let me know he was called out and that it would be a bit. Dom can only do so much but yeah he's got friends from his military days he'll probably call on to get the ball rolling," Laura said on a sigh.

"So basically we're goners no matter what since no one would be looking for us," Danika repeated.

"No, you haven't met our Captain. That's one scary bitch and she has no problems strong-arming the political powers that be to send in someone to get us. Just hang in there, Danika. If they do come in and take you don't give them the pleasure of knowing they are hurting you, no matter how much it hurts. Don't cry, don't scream out, don't give them any reaction, and they will lose interest. They want to break your will and if you give them any reaction it eggs them on because you're a fighter," Cortez stated with strong conviction.

Laura sighed. "This is all my fault. I shouldn't have pissed Ackerman off."

Cortez opened one good eye. "Don't you dare start that shit, Laura. These guys got pissed the minute we started looking for these girls. We did our job and we will continue to do our job. We may die in the line of duty but at least we fought for these girls despite the fact there are bad badges out there being paid off to look the other way."

A short time later, Mendoza walked into the room with a big grin on his face. "Ah lovely senoritas, which one should I take now? Will it be one of our lovely young guests to start their training for my dick or hand them over to one of my men to have their fun? Maybe I should take the lovely Detective Pratt and have my fun with you?"

"Fuck you, asshole. Do your worst. But you won't break me," Laura spat out.

Mendoza laughed as he grabbed Laura's arm and dragged her out of the room. He dragged her into a room four doors down from where he held them. "Let's see how long it takes you to beg for your life or that of your partner? This should be fun."

Laura never saying a word, only glared at him. Mendoza started to shift from foot to foot, getting uncomfortable with her staring at him. Laura knew he didn't like it when a woman appeared to be on an even field with him. She knew he was uncomfortable and basked in the aura of that fact.

Laura didn't know what all they did to Cortez, but she had a strong feeling she was about to find out. Mendoza advanced toward her and smacked her hard across the face with his open palm. "You think you're so much better than me, don't you puta?"

Laura didn't say anything. She just turned her head back toward Mendoza and glared at him. She wasn't going to give him the satisfaction of a response. She knew what he wanted and she wasn't going to give in to it. No matter how much it hurt.

Mendoza came back at her again this time punching her with a closed fist, knocking her over, chair and all. Laura grunted from the force of the blow and the hard fall. She closed her eyes and bit her lip hard to keep from screaming out, which enraged Mendoza even more.

Huffing and growling, Mendoza came over and kicked her legs which were tied to the chair she had been sitting on over and over again. Mendoza stopped, breathing heavily as he stumbled back becoming angry that Laura didn't scream out once. Looking over at the thug behind him, he jerked his head toward the table.

Laura was picked up, ropes cut from the chair, dragged over to the table, and once again strapped down. "Let's see how well you can handle this, you bitch." Laura just stared at the thug not saying a work or giving any indication that she was scared.

Laura was petrified. Despite the fact that she

loved water and the beaches, which goes hand in hand with living in San Diego and being involved with a SEAL, her biggest fear had always been drowning. She panicked when Mendoza placed the rag over her mouth and nose as the man poured a bucket of water slowly over her face. When they removed the rag, Laura started coughing and spitting water at the men and gasping for air. Mendoza and his henchman continued waterboarding Laura for over an hour, each time making her gasp for air, coughing and spitting up water.

Mendoza becoming angrier with the lack of response from Laura, removed her from the table and dragged her over to hang her from the meat hook by her tied hands, dangling from the ceiling in the middle of the room. He tore Laura's shirt off of her body and smirked. He balled his hands into fists and spoke to Thug Moron in Spanish. Laura watched as Thug Moron walked out of the room. Mendoza walked around the room for a few moments, then turned before he headed straight up to Laura and punched her hard into her stomach causing her to gasp from the surprise punch.

Mendoza started laughing as he threw some more punches to her stomach and kidneys, walking around her in circles as he did so. Thug Moron walked back into the room with a whip, a baseball bat, and carrying a car battery with cables. Laura gulped seeing the items in his hand, but the vision was short-lived as Mendoza started hitting her again.

"I want to know who you talked to about your investigation into the arcade, Detective. You can give it to me now or I can cause you so much pain. Either way, you will tell me what I want to know."

"Ok, ok, I'll talk. Shit. Ok, I went to my Captain and told him what we knew and then he went to his boss and it was decided to put pressure on Ackerman."

"Very good. Now what is your Captain's name?" smiled Mendoza on the win.

"Shit, he'll have my ass in a sling. His name is Captain Kirk of the Starship Enterprise and his boss is Star Lord," Laura said, with a straight face.

Mendoza roared as he pummeled Laura in the stomach and kidney area harder. He stepped back after several hard punches and ordered his guy to hook up the battery and cables and to get the hose. "You think you're so funny, puta. But you've only made things harder for yourself."

For the next two hours Mendoza kept good on his promise to cause her immerse pain. She was shocked with the cables connected to the car battery, she was beaten from head to toe, whipped, water-boarded and beaten some more.

For four days, Cortez and Laura fought with everything they had against Mendoza and his men. They believed that as long as Mendoza was focused on them, they wouldn't touch the girls, they were protected because Mendoza was occupied with them. But, they didn't know who much longer they could keep it up.

7

"Matthew, I need to get up and get ready for work," laughed Caroline. "You're going to be late if you don't get your shower." Caroline turned over and kissed Matthew 'Wolf' Steel and got out of bed.

"We can conserve water and shower together." Wolf said, as he got out of bed and chased his wife into the bathroom. Just as he got to the door, his phone went off. Grabbing his phone, he answered.

"Wolf."

"Wolf, gather your team and get into the office. We've got a mission," Commander Patrick Hurt ordered.

"Yes sir, we'll be there within the hour." Wolf hung up and sent a secured text to the rest of the men on his SEAL team to be at Commander Hurt's office within the hour.

"Sorry, babe, seems like we have a mission." Wolf kissed Caroline deeply and passionately, then got a quick shower to dress for his meeting with the team.

One hour later, Wolf, Cookie, Abe, Dude, Mozart, and Benny were gathered in Commander Hurt's office. "Gentlemen, sorry to cut your morning short, but we've got a hot one. Two female detectives from our of Riverton County Sheriff's Department, Human Trafficking Task Force, were kidnapped approximately four days ago. They were investigating the disappearance of four underage girls, Tabitha Jennings, Danika Star, Juanita Sanchez, and Farzooh Nadinaez. It's believed that the owner of the arcade killed the kid that worked for him to draw the two Detectives, Laura 'Red' Pratt and Tarilyn 'Taz' Cortez, to him, two San Diego PD officers were also killed in the process."

"Why kill the SDPD officers but not the detectives? That doesn't make sense," Hunter 'Cookie' Knox said.

"No, it doesn't. Their Captain believes it has to do with the investigation itself. They apparently caught the eye of the man who wanted the girls so he ordered Ackerman to take the detectives, as well."

Hurt's phone started ringing. "Hurt. Yes sir, the team is here. They just arrived and I was giving them the basic rundown. Yes sir, give me a minute to put you on speaker. You're on speaker now, sir. Gentlemen, President Lyman wants to speak with you personally."

"Gentlemen, thank you for arriving promptly. I'm sorry to have cut into your morning but I wanted the best on this mission and Senator Lytle tells me you're the best. Gentlemen, I owe these two women my life so I'm pulling out all the stops to get them rescued. They saved my daughter when she was kidnapped by a rogue Secret Service Agent a couple of years ago. They've kept in touch with her through it all and made sure she knew she wasn't alone. My daughter is distraught when she learned that these two in particular are missing. I want them found and brought home, along with those four young girls. Any questions?"

"No, sir. We will get them back no problems, sir," Wolf replied in the affirmative.

The phone disconnected when Kason 'Benny' Sawyer pipped up, "So these girls know the President of the United States?"

"More like the president's daughter did," Christopher 'Abe' Powers said with respect. "So these two are part of a task force that focuses on Human Trafficking? How come we've never heard of them?"

"Because gentlemen, my team operates quietly," Captain Irby said stepping to the front of the room. "That's why they are effective. They started out as a pilot team to see how well it worked with all the issues of victims falling through the cracks of the system. We've been very successful after we got our feet planted. We are still working through the initial trial and error phase. I'm Captain Katherine Irby, the head of the Human Trafficking Task Force. I was asked by your Commander to bring over what you would need to go after my girls. They are strong and they are tough. Bring them home to me gentlemen. Commander, here are the files you requested. I know I could have emailed them, but I needed to look you and your men in the face. I needed know that your team will bring my girls home. They are family. It took us four days to get this far, we won't stop until they are home, even if that means going against every protocol and going to Mexico to recover them ourselves."

"These men are the best. Not sure how you got in here, but thank you. We will bring them home, Captain. I'll have my assistant escort you out."

Turning back to the men, Hurt continued

briefing the team. "Ok men, you're going into Mexico. The man they are the guest of, and I use the term lightly, one Francisco Mendoza. These women pissed off the head of the Mendoza cartel. He risked everything to have these women taken. This is everything the department and our intel has on him. Go kick ass and bring them home." Hurt dismissed the men after passing out the information prepared for the team.

Wolf and the team grabbed their gear and headed to the plane to get in the air and go over their mission. "Ok guys, we have two adult females and four minor females. I think we all can agree that the two detectives won't leave without the kids unless they are in a body bag. So we need to be prepared for any resistance. They can help keep the girls calm if they are able to."

"Shit, from what this file says, Detective Pratt has a brother that was former Delta Force. Cortez is also former Army. These two are military affiliated in some way, shape, or form so they will fight with everything they have. I think our main focus will be on keeping the four younger girls calm," Abe stated, skimming through his file.

"If these two are as good as the President and their Captain stated, I wouldn't be surprised if we wind up finding them fighting their captors when we get there. They sound like the type that would do anything and everything to keep the focus on them, just to make sure the girls are left alone," Sam 'Mozart' Reed put in his two cents.

"Using Mozart's logic, then we can assume that we may be carrying one if not both out," Faulkner 'Dude' Cooper commented.

"Agreed, so be prepared for them to be fighting off anyone and everyone if they are able to, but the strong chance we will have to be carrying one or two out," Wolf remarked.

"Do we know which area we are going into? According to intel, Mendoza has two compounds where he regularly stays. He's very rarely seen out in the public unless he's going from one to the other. How do we know which one he's at, not even intel can give us a general idea," Benny chimed in.

"According to intel, which compound shows the most activity right now?" Wolf asked Benny.

"Since Mendoza is the head of the Mendoza cartel, they pretty much run everything from Ensenada to San Elequoi. He has a compound in Ensenada and San Elequoi about forty miles south. From what intel shows, the most activity is around San

Elequoi, but it doesn't jive with the activity that's going on in Ensenada."

"Shit, this guy runs that much? That's a lot of territory. We don't have the ability to go through both of those. If we hit the wrong one, our element of surprise is gone. We'll be sitting ducks and they will up the guards for the other. Wait, you said the activity doesn't jive with each other, what do you mean Benny?" Mozart questioned.

"It means that one or the other usually has more activity than the other. San Elequoi has the most activity right now, making it look like they are all there. But there's small amount of movement coming out of Ensenada which is unusual other than the small number of guards that would still patrol the area to keep the home protected, but this looks like more than that. Mendoza is married with kids, right?"

"What if the wife and kids are in San Elequoi, which would make sense for him to have the family away while he's entertaining our targets at the Ensenada compound? That would make sense to me. These two are enough to cause a ruckus and draw attention. They are fighters. My gut says they are the Ensenada compound while he sent the wife and family to the San Elequoi place," Abe declared.

"I agree with Abe - Ensenada. What about the rest of you men?" Wolf asked the rest of the team.

After getting the nods from the rest of the team, they alerted the pilot they were ready while they prepped their gear ready and worked out how they were going to go in and rescue the victims.

Six hours later, the team arrived at the outskirts of the Ensenada compound and started their observation. After hour two, they finally saw movement in the compound. "Well, there's Mendoza's top man. Son of a bitch, what is that he's dragging?" Mozart whispered into his mic.

"Fuck, that's one of the detectives. They worked her over good," Dude fumed.

All of the sudden, the man went down, the female they were dragging jumped on top of him fighting, three more men came out of the building to assist their fallen thug. The men cringed when they saw one of the men backhand her. "Enough, they are going to kill her. Take them out, Benny. Let's go," Wolf ordered.

Wolf and the team took off and took out the four thugs. Laura whirled around after grabbing the thug's gun she'd been fighting with and turned to where the shots came from, aiming at the figures running her way. "Stay right there, asshole, or I'll blow your head off your shoulders."

"Detective Laura Pratt?" Wolf asked, raising his hands in the air.

"Who the fuck are you?" Laura responded tersely.

"Ma'am, I'm Lt. Matthew 'Wolf' Steel with the United States Navy, we're SEALs. We're the good guys. We're here to get you, Detective Cortez and the young girls that you were trying to find back to safety. You have a lot of people creating hell to get you guys back home," Wolf calmly told Laura. "This is Mozart our team medic. He can look you over really quick and then check on Cortez and the girls. Anyone else beside you hurt?"

"Cortez is pretty bad off. They've focused on us, which is what we wanted. Mendoza finally caught on to what we were doing. I think we pissed him off with the Captain Kirk and Star Lord references. Asshole on the ground here got pissed with the Jabba the Hutt reference. Damn pussy. The girls are in good shape to hike, scared but unharmed. I'm ok, I can make it. Cortez is strong. Probably a broken rib or two but can walk."

"Ma'am, I'm Mozart. Where does it hurt the most?"

"Dude, if you call me ma'am one more time I'm going to punch you despite the fact you're rescuing me. Makes me sound like I'm old. I'm ok, really. Yeah, I don't look it. I know they worked me over good and I'm slow right now with everything aching, but I'm fine. My concern is my partner. Check her out. I'll be ok. I promise you won't have to carry me out." Laura started to walk away and stumbled.

Dude caught her with a growl, "You're not fine. You can barely stand. You need to be honest and tell us where you're injured. And for the record detective, his name is Mozart, I'm Dude. Now please tell us what hurts so we can get you guys out of here safely."

"I thought there were more of you? Why are you two the only ones here? Where did the others go?"

"They went to search the compound for Mendoza and make sure there's no more risk to you and your partner, that way we can get you all out of here fast. Now please tell me what injuries you have," Dude asked quietly.

Laura looked at Dude and sighed. "What is it with SEALs and the alpha gene? I'm ok. Yeah, my leg is a little unstable because they took a baseball bat to the knee and ankle but I can walk. Just give me a few minutes. I need to get to Cortez to make sure they didn't do anything to her while they had me in the room they used as their torture chamber. I need to make sure all four girls are still in there with her."

Laura led Mozart and Dude to where the rest of the group was last seen. When they opened the door, Cortez was ready to attack before she saw Laura come forward. "Taz, it's ok. They are the good guys. This is Dude and this is Mozart. They are SEALs coming to rescue us. Are all four girls here?"

"Yeah, Mendoza came in to get one of them, saying that it was time to take out the trash and head lugnut would be back to get me. But all of the sudden he ran out like the hounds of hell were on his ass."

"Probably because the asshole knew he was next. These guys took out four of his guards, including Jabba. Are you ready to get the hell out of here?"

"I'm good, Red. Let's get these girls ready to go," Cortez heaved out.

Cortez and Laura got the girls together and explained who Mozart and Dude were and said that they could trust these men to get them home to their parents. Juanita and Tabitha each got on one side of Cortez to assist her while Danika and Farzooh glued themselves to Laura.

"We are ready to go, sir. I am Danika. Farz and I

will help you with Detective Pratt. Juanita and Tabbie have Detective Cortez. They didn't abandon us so we refuse to do the same to them. We'll make sure we help them keep up."

Dude nodded and lead the group out of the room. They met up with Wolf and the rest of the team. Introductions were made. "Mendoza is nowhere to be found. It seems like the four guys we took out are all that's here."

"Cortez here just told us he was in the room with them when they heard the shots. He probably has an extraction plan in place. We saw no cars leaving so he's got to be close," Mozart reported.

"We need to get the hell out of here. Ladies, how good are you to hump it out of here on foot. Our extraction point is about 5 miles out," Wolf asked Laura and Cortez.

"Lt., we're good to go. We know we look the opposite of that, but I promise we won't slow you down. Let's do this," Cortez informed the team.

Wolf and Abe led everyone out of the compound, Mozart and Dude in the middle assisting with the precious cargo, Benny and Cookie taking up the rear. The men had to admit they were impressed with the women's determination to watch over the young girls They kept a close eye on the two detectives knowing they put themselves in harm's way for the last four days to make sure the girls weren't touched. Cookie was very impressed and appreciative of what the two women sacrificed, even if they didn't talk about what happened to them.

At mile four, something didn't feel right. They had to take it slow since the girls had shorter legs, tiring easily and the detective's injuries. Wolf turned around and nodded at the men, Abe and Benny took off. Wolf motioned for the women to have a rest and handed them a canteen with some water in it. "How are you holding up?"

"We're fine. Just ready to get out of here, I want to hug my son and be able to tuck him into bed tonight," Laura responded to Wolf.

"You need to get that leg checked out, Red. I know you don't want to admit it to these guys, but you've been babying that damn leg since we left the compound. These guys don't know you but I do," Cortez spoke up, worried about Laura's leg.

Laura went to stand up when a shot rang out. Laura flew back, landing hard on the ground. Wolf and the other SEALs went into action getting the girls covered. Cortez went to Laura and started dragging her along with Wolf. Abe and Benny came running back giving cover fire.

"Where the hell did that come from? We need to get these girls out of here now," Mozart growled at Wolf.

"How is she?" Wolf asked Mozart.

"Not good. They got her in the upper left chest area. She's lucky she moved the way she did or it would have been a heart shot. We need to get her out of here fast or she won't make it."

"Red, hold on please. You've got Cody to tuck in and Highlander to wait for when he comes back from his mission. You promised him you'd be ok. Damn it, fight," Cortez pleaded.

"Highlander?" Mozart questioned Cortez.

"Yes. She's been seeing, living with, or whatever you SEALs call it with Lt. Joe MacLeod. He's deployed right now on assignment."

"Detective Pratt, you need to hold on like your partner says. You have a SEAL to get home to. He won't be happy if you die on our watch. Help a brother out and fight so he doesn't cap our asses." Cookie held onto Laura's hands to let her know she was surrounded.

"She's one of ours. Damn it, MacLeod is going to be pissed if she doesn't make it. What do we do, Wolf? We have to get her out of here if she's going to make it." Cookie watched Dude and Mozart work on Laura to stabilize her.

"She's his. Lander came by just before his mission to ask if it was ok for him to introduce her to us. He was hesitant because of Fiona finding out her background, and I couldn't understand why. Now I do. Caroline and I were planning on doing a cookout for the teams once they got back if we weren't shipped out. We need to find this shooter so we can get her out of here. You and Abe are with me. Have Dude, Benny and Mozart on the girls while they get Laura stabilized and ready to go after we dispatch this son of a bitch. We have to get her home now." Wolf gave the orders, as he, Abe, and Cookie took off to find the shooter.

Thirty minutes later they returned back to the group satisfied with their mission to find the shooter and dispatch him. When they met up with the rest of the group, Mozart had taped Laura's wound to help slow the bleeding. Dude picked up Laura and carried her the rest of the way to their extraction point.

8

Laura woke up looking around the room she was in. She saw Raso in the chair at the far end of the bed talking with Cody and helping him color and Dom standing near the window talking to someone on her other side. She slowly turned her head to the left and saw Joe sitting in the chair holding her hand.

"Joe?"

"Hey beautiful, boy am I so glad te see ye eyes." Joe leaned over and kissed her forehead.

"Where am I? Last thing I remember is following Lt. Steel and his team to their extraction point, then stopping, because they were worried about Cortez and I, then nothing. Oh my God, Cortez, is she ok? Where is she?" Laura started to get worked up.

"Baby, it's ok, calm down. She's ok. She's just

down the hall. Diesel and Rameriez are with her. She's ok. How are ye? Are ye in any pain? The surgery te remove the bullet went smooth. They were more worried about ye bleeding out since there was nae vest on." Joe rubbed Laura's arm.

"Yeah bad guys find it kind of hard to allow their victims to wear a bulletproof vest while they beat your ass and stuff, it kind of defeats the purpose," snapped Laura.

"Well at least ye didn't lose your fire, lass. Now are ye in any pain? Is there anything that ye need?" Joe tried again a little firmer.

"I'm fine, Joe. How long have you been home?"

"I got home the same day Wolf and the guys went te get ye. They had just taken off a few hours before we landed. I found out when they came back that ye and Cortez were their mission."

"The girls, are they ok? They will need counseling. They weren't touched but they were still traumatized with everything else going on," Laura whispered to Joe.

Raso walked over to the bed. "The girls are ok. They have contacted the Captain several times to make sure you're ok. They've asked to be able to come see you and Taz when you're ready for visitors. They are already scheduled for their recommended counseling sessions. So you and Taz need to focus on getting better. How are you feeling there, partner?"

"I'm fine. A little sore, but it's manageable. I don't want any more drugs. I hate how they make me feel."

"Ack lass, I'm here. Ye need te rest and get better. If ye are in pain, take the meds so ye can rest," Joe soothed.

Laura's brother, Dominick, chimed in as he crossed the room, "Sis, I have Cody. One more night at my place isn't a problem. I love having the squirt when you guys let me. Focus on getting better so you're out in the next day or two. Cody and I have this. I love you." Dom held his sisters hand as he kissed her forehead. "Come on, squirt. Give your mom a kiss and we'll go get some ice cream."

"Yay!!" Cody jumped up from his spot and ran over to Laura's bed and climbed up. He enthusiastically started signing to Laura, "I love you mommy. I'm glad you're home. I missed you. Can't wait for you to come home, love you." Cody leaned up and kissed Laura then hopped down grabbing his Uncle Dom's hand.

Raso decided to leave with them so Laura could

get some rest, plus she wanted to check on Cortez, too.

When Dom, Cody, and Raso left, Joe and Laura were alone in the room. "You can go home if you want. I know those chairs can't be comfortable. I'm sure there's things that you need to do – don't stop just because I'm in here."

"Ye just don't get it, do ye lass. I'm here with ye. There's nowhere else I'd rather be. The chair is fine. I'm nae leaving ye, love *tha goal agam ort*."

Laura started crying, clinging to Joe's hand. "I love you, too."

"Wolf and the guys all came by to check on ye earlier while ye were asleep. Ye and Cortez impressed them with how determined ye were to protect the girls. They were a little miffed that ye didn't tell them that ye were a SEAL's girl, though." Joe chuckled.

"I didn't want special attention or the focus to be taken off of the girls' safety. I didn't want them to risk their lives to save me just because I was your girlfriend, Joe. I love you and would fight to get back home to you, but those girls were priority. If it meant my life for theirs, then that's what it would have been. I know that's not what you want to hear, but that's the truth of it."

Joe sighed. "I know, lass. I knew that as soon as I found out what happened that's what ye and Cortez would do. As much as I hate the idea, I wouldn't have expected anything less from ye." Joe leaned over and kissed Laura. "Get some sleep, lass. I'll be here if ye need me."

"Will you cuddle with me? I don't think I can handle sleeping alone, even if you're in the chair next to me."

"Aye lass, scoot over." Joe climbed into the bed with Laura, bringing her back to his front and wrapping his arms around her tight. They both needed the reassurance after her ordeal.

———

SHORTLY AFTER SHE had fallen asleep there was a knock on the door. Wolf, Dude, and Cookie walked into the room. "How is she? We stopped by to see Cortez and another teammate Raso said she was awake," Wolf whispered.

"She's ok. Refusing the pain meds because she doesn't want te be out of it if she's needed. She's tough. Thank ye guys for going in and bringing them home."

"Why didn't she tell us she was yours, Joe? We

didn't know until Cortez was telling her that you would be pissed she got shot after she promised to stay in one piece," Dude asked.

"The truth? She didn't want ye to put her first. She knew that we had a code that if one of our women were in danger, they were a priority to get back to our brother. She wanted the focus te be on the girls and getting them back te their parents. If they were in any danger, she and Cortez both would have put their lives on the line to make sure they made it home, as ye can see from the looks of both of them." Joe brushed Laura's hair back and kissed the side of her head.

"She's definitely a SEAL wife." Cookie chuckled. "I have to admit I admired that she and Cortez fought tooth and nail to make sure those girls weren't touch. Very rarely does that happen. I'm surprised Mendoza didn't touch the girls while they were out of it. Have they talked to anyone about what happened?"

"According to Raso, Cortez hasn't said anything. Laura just woke up a little while ago. Hasn't really said much other than why she didn't identify herself as mine. She did ask if you guys made it out ok since she didn't remember much after you guys stopped to rest." Joe started to get up so he could talk with the guys better when Laura started to whimper.

"It's ok, we just wanted to stop by and check on them. Caroline says we're going to have the cookout for the teams two weeks from tomorrow. That will give Laura time to heal. Caroline wants to invite the rest of her team, as well. Oh, before I forget, there's a big meeting for all the teams that are stateside tomorrow morning. Hurt wanted me to let you know to be there at 0900." Wolf nodded and walked out of the room with Cookie following him.

"You've got a good one there, Highlander. She saved Wolf's life out there. While she may be yours, she's ours, too. If you ever need anything, let us know." Dude nodded and started to leave.

"Dude, what do ye mean she saved Wolf? He never said anything," Joe called out, stopping him.

"The shot was meant to take out Wolf from the angle that the bullet hit her. Had she not stood up and turned the way she did, it would have hit Wolf or been a heart shot on her. Take good care of her or you'll have one of us kicking your ass." Dude left, after one last look at Laura.

Joe lay back down and pulled Laura in closer. Hearing that it would have either been her or his brother-in-arms taken down with that shot, he thanked God she had turned at just the right angle. He needed to call his brother Mike tomorrow, to give him the update on Laura and Cortez. His transfer from Bragg to Hood prevented him from coming out here and seeing for himself. Bryson and Marcus were both deployed or they would have moved heaven and hell to be here beside him. His croie had touched every single person in his family's heart, both his blood and his brothers-in-arms. There was no way he would let anything happen to his heart. Making sure she was covered, he snuggled up behind her more and closed his eyes and tried to get some sleep.

9

____

Laura woke up to find herself alone in the room with a note on the bedside table next to her with a rose laying across it. Joe had written her to let her know he would be back after a meeting that his Commander had called for all the teams. She sighed and laid her head back against the pillow. She heard a knock on the door and saw it open. Standing there were two unfamiliar women.

"Hi, I'm Caroline, Matthew's wife. This is Fiona, Hunter's wife. May we come in?"

"Matthew? Hunter? I'm sorry I don't know who that is."

"I'm sorry they probably used their nicknames. Matthew is Wolf and Hunter is Cookie. Sorry, we call them by their given names despite them telling everyone their nicknames." Caroline laughed and walked further into the room. "We wanted to come by and see how you were doing. See if you needed anything."

"Oh, Wolf and Cookie. Hi. Yeah come in. I'm ok. Hoping they let me go home today. We shall see." Laura smiled weakly. She was always nervous around new people, especially these women since they were the wives of men that Joe worked with and called friends.

"Wolf, Cookie, and Dude came by last night to see how you and your partner were doing. You've officially been adopted by the whole team, so that makes you our sister, too. Just know, if you or Cortez ever need anything, all you have to do is call. I know you don't know us just yet, but we'd like to fix that." Caroline went on, "I'm having a cookout in two weeks from today. I would love for you and your team to be there. You'll get to meet the other wives."

"Oh..."

Before Laura could finish her sentence her door opened. In walked her mother Kathy and one of her stepsisters, Jennifer. Laura tensed up and gripped the bed covers. "Mother, Jennifer, how did you find out I was here? I know Dom didn't tell you where I was."

"Just because you and your brother decided that you are orphans doesn't mean I can't find out about you two. I do have my own resources, you know. I'm not an invalid where my children are concerned," Kathy sneered. "Now where is my grandson? I hope you're not expecting that squid to take care of my grandson. Cody isn't his. Lord, Laura Renee, I raised you better than that. He needs to be with his father, raised by a man who knows what he's doing."

"First of all mother, where my son is none of your concern - you don't give a rat's ass about him any other day of the week so don't start now. Second, you know damn good and well Jonathan doesn't want him, especially since he's with his prostitute, the one you deemed ok for him to have on the side while I was supposed to be grateful he was going to stay married to me. As for Joe, he's more of a man than Jonathan ever has been or ever will be and loves Cody as if he was his own son. So if he wants to take care of him while I'm in here or while I'm at work, I would be one hell of a lucky woman."

"Mom, let's just go. It's obvious that whoever took her didn't want her either. I don't know why we are here. She will never change and realize she's a nobody. Maybe when this man's command or friends realize what kind of woman she is, he'll wake up and realize his mistake. You did your best in raising the ungrateful whale. Hell, he's probably out banging some other women right now just so he can tolerate being near her," Jennifer murmured to her stepmother.

"Excuse me, I don't know who you are, but you don't know Lt. MacLeod like we do. We are his friends. Just like Laura said, he's more man than you could ever dream of meeting. And I know for a fact he's not with another woman, so your jealousy is actually comical. All he ever talks about is his love for Laura and her son Cody. In fact, he calls Cody his son. If Laura and her brother didn't call you to tell you where she was or what was going on, it's obvious they don't want you here. I strongly suggest that you leave. Call next time to see if you are wanted before you come here again." Caroline was fuming.

Kathy and Jennifer sneered at the three women and walked out of the room without a further word. Laura looked at Caroline, "Thank you, I appreciate it. I think I'm going to take a nap now until the doctor comes in and decides what the plans are. Thanks for coming by." Laura started to shut down.

"Don't listen to them, Laura. Wolf and the guys would go to the ends of the earth to protect those they deem theirs. So would Joe. That's part of being with a SEAL - you don't just get one, you get them all. You also get us too, and I know for a fact what your mother said was not true. We may have just met, but you're one of us, through the good and the bad. I meant what I said, here's my number, you call if you need anything. Fiona's is on there, too." Caroline laid a piece of paper on the table next to the hospital bed and leaned over giving Laura a one-sided hug, followed by one from Fiona.

Later that day, Laura was set to be released and sent home to recuperate with strict instructions to remain on bed rest for the next several days. She called her brother to come and get her. She was still drained and upset about the visit from her mom and stepsister. She had always known her mother hated her, but she could never understand why. Not even Dom knew what the issue was. Laura felt that her parents hated her since she wasn't perfect due to her hearing impairment that had her wearing two hearing aids. While her body type didn't fit her mother's image of perfect, Joe had helped her find acceptance and happiness in herself. She fought to get her job in the sheriff's department as well as the task force and had never regretted it. Even if she didn't have her parents' approval, she'd always had Dom as her biggest supporter in life, now second to

Joe. She was eternally grateful she was close with her brother.

After helping her into her house, Dom looked at Laura with a concerned look in his eyes, "Hey sis, you've been really quiet since you called to ask me to get you. What's up, squirtle?" Dom hugged his baby sister.

"What makes you think something is wrong? I'm fine. Just tired that's all," Laura reacted.

"Because you were quiet, which is unlike you. You didn't want me to call Joe and let him know I picked you up, plus the nurse said mom and Jennifer were there and ordered to get out." Dom looked Laura in the eyes as he said the last part.

"I'm fine, Dom. Just mom being the same usual snarky bitch she always is. Only this time she had Maria Jr. with her. Same shit, different day. Bitching about the fact we didn't 'notify' her of the name tarnish aka me making the news for some reason or another so she could show her face at the country club. Wonder what sob story she gave to be able to stay there. I think mom's pimping Jennifer out now that Maria is in the wind. They actually tried to sell some bullshit story that Joe was out screwing some chick just so he could be in the same room with me. What's even more hilarious is the twit brigade tried to claim that if his friends and command met me, they would tell him he was an idiot for dating me. Stupid bitch."

"They are just pissed because you're happy for once in your life and theirs is falling apart. Joe loves the hell out of you and Cody. Hell, he even came by and took him to school before going to his meeting. A man doesn't do that if it's a pity relationship, no matter what anyone says. His friends are just as protective of you as Joe and I are. You and Cortez made one hell of an impression on that entire SEAL team, and it wasn't because you're Joe's girlfriend. Sis, they told Joe themselves if he ever hurt you, they would kick his ass. I heard that with my own ears. Don't let mom and the twisted sister reject ruin that for you," Dom fumed.

"Twisted sister reject?" Laura sputtered out.

"Seriously, have you seen the makeup? I think they had the same makeup artist or she watched too many videos and did it in the wrong language or something. She makes Tammy Faye Baker's makeup seem natural. Hell, a clown looks more natural than hers. Duhhhh." Dom made a face as he was joking with Laura.

Laura broke into a laugh then punched her

brother's arm. "That hurt, asshole, and you do know Tammy Faye Baker is dead, right? Knobtard."

"Sorry, didn't mean to cause you pain, but you just hit me, you evil meanie. I'm going to go home and cry. And yes, I know she's dead, that's why the makeup would be more natural than Jennifer's " Dom laughed as he hugged his sister. "Do you need anything else before I go? Need big brother to tuck you in?"

"Ew, gross dude. Did they teach you that gross shit in Delta? What's your old teammates name again? I'm going to call him and tell him that you need your ass kicked, perv." Laura laughed hugging her brother back.

After Dom left, Laura locked up and for the first time, she actually was afraid of being home alone. She laid down on the couch and before she knew it, she was asleep. She woke up to feeling fingers rubbing against her cheek. She jumped up then groaned in pain, grabbing her ribs.

"Aye lass, it's just me. It's ok. I'm sorry I didn't mean te scare ye." Joe held his hands up while he spoke softly to Laura to give her a chance to relax.

"Joe? I thought you were at work?"

"Aye lass, I was. It's a little after six. Ye slept the afternoon away. I went by the hospital, but they said ye had been released earlier. Why didn't ye call te tell me that ye had been released?

"I meant to send you a text after I got settled. I didn't want to bother you while you were at work. I'm sorry I didn't realize I had fallen asleep. Give me just a minute and I'll make dinner." Laura started to get up but Joe put his hand on her shoulder to keep her in place.

"Nae lass, don't worry about dinner. Ye need ye rest. I can manage a simple meal for the three of us."

"Three of us? Who else is coming? Joe, I'm not in the mood or condition for more company," Laura fretted.

"Nae lass, nae company. It's just ye, Cody, and myself. He sent me a text asking if I could come and get him te bring him home so he could help take care of his mum. He's at the kitchen table doing his homework right now."

"Oh. Oh my god, what kind of mother am I when I didn't even consider getting my own kid." Laura buried her head in her pillow on the couch and started crying.

Joe pulled her into his arms and gently sat down on the couch and let Laura cry. He soothed her hair from her forehead and kissed her. "Lass, ye are a damn good mum. That boy loves ye. Ye needed some alone time te get some rest. It will be ok, love." Joe kissed her forehead again and just held Laura in his arms.

———

Joe fixed a simple dinner of soup and grilled cheese, cleaned the kitchen, helped Cody with the rest of his homework, and got him ready for bed. He wouldn't admit it out loud but he was worried about Laura. She was kind of withdrawn into herself, wouldn't talk about what she gone through while in Mexico.

Bed time finally rolled around. Joe was hesitant on what to do. "Lass, time te get in the bed. Need me te help ye?"

"Huh? Oh, um no, I'm ok I can make it." Laura got up and went to the bathroom.

A short time later she came out of the bathroom and started getting ready for bed. She looked at the bed, to Joe, and then back again. When Joe came up behind her to wrap his arms around her, she froze. When Joe started to back away, she turned around and grabbed his hand.

"Sorry, just a knee jerk reaction, I don't know why I'm doing that. I know you won't hurt me. Please forgive me?" Laura said as tears welled up in her eyes.

Joe pulled her into his arms and held her tight. "It's ok, love. I know. I just didn't want te cause ye stress. Would it be better if I slept on the couch for a few nights until ye are ready te sleep next te me?"

Laura froze and dropped her arms from his waist. "Is that what you want? Did I do something wrong?" Laura started to back up away from Joe.

"Laura, stop!" Joe grabbed her by the shoulders to keep her in place. "Ye have done nothing wrong. No, it is nae what I want te do. I want te be in our bed with ye in my arms. I want te fall asleep with my arms around ye. I want te wake up with my arms around ye hearing ye snore away next te me. But I can tell ye are a little scared right now and I don't want te cause ye fear."

Laura stared at Joe as he spoke. She started breathing again and stepped forward, wrapping her arms around his waist. "No I don't want you to sleep on the couch. I want your arms around me, too. I need to know you're there next to me if I get scared. Please don't leave me."

Joe cradled Laura's face in his hands and leaned down and gently kissed her. He tasted her lips, licking and nibbling her lower lip then slipping his tongue inside her mouth when she opened up under him. Laura hands roamed from his waist up to his chest and into his hair holding him tight. The kiss became heated, a mating of the tongues that were torn apart and reunited.

Without breaking contact, Joe picked Laura up, wrapping her legs around his waist and walked them toward the bed. He laid Laura down, devouring her mouth while his left hand moved up and down her thigh at his waist. They came up for air as Joe moved his lips down her neck to her collar bone and nipped her shoulder.

"Fuck lass, I've missed ye so much." Joe took her arms and raised them above her head with one hand as he raised her shirt to her neck so that he could tease her nipples.

Laura tried to move her hand to touch Joe but she couldn't. Joe kept her hand where it was while he feasted on her nipple. Laura kept trying to move her hand and started to panic. When she couldn't move her hands, she started fighting and hyperventilating.

"Hey, hey, hey, lass it's ok." Joe let Laura's hands go and sat up beside her as she scrambled to the top of the bed. Laura wrapped her arms around her middle. "Are ye ok, Laura? Did I do something wrong?"

"No, I'm sorry. Joe. I just panicked when I couldn't move my hands to touch you. I'm so sorry." Laura started to sob.

"Lass, it's ok." Joe slowly moved toward Laura and pulled her into his arms. "I'm the one who is sorry. I should nae have moved so fast te make love te ye. I should be the one apologizing te ye."

Joe slowly brought Laura down off the headboard and laid down on the bed with her. He brought her back to his front and curled his arms around her to make sure her hands were free so she didn't feel trapped again. He wished that he could find that son of a bitch, Mendoza, and put a bullet in his head. Brushing Laura's hair back off her face, he leaned down and kissed her cheek. They would get through this, come hell or high water they would get through this together.

10

____

Joe and Laura fell into a routine for the next week. She took Cody to school, cleaned the house, picked Cody up from school, made dinner, and then went to bed. Laura knew she was just going through the motions of the day. At night she would get a shower and climb into bed. She at least stayed awake until he got into the bed and talked with her as he pulled her into him and held her. She knew he didn't know what else to do.

While Laura was cleaning the house several days after being released, she heard a knock on her front door. Answering the door, she was surprised by her visitor. "Fiona, hi, I didn't know you were coming by."

"I know I should have called but wanted to come by and see how you were doing. Mind if I come in?"

"No come in, sorry, my manners went down the drain. Would you like something to drink? I have water, tea, and wine."

"Tea is fine." Fiona sat at the table in the kitchen while Laura got them both some iced tea. "How have you been?"

Laura sighed. "Taking one day at a time. I'm ready to go back to work - so tired of feeling like I have nothing to do. I think this house will be happy I've gone back to work, too. There's nothing left for me to clean and yet I'm still doing it. I think once I'm back in uniform and on the job, I'll be fine."

"Have you talked to anyone about what happened? I mean to Joe, Cortez, your captain, or a professional."

"No. Captain Irby wants us to talk to the department shrink, but I'm not comfortable with her. She's nasally and judgmental." Laura chuckled.

Fiona pulled a card out of her purse and handed it to Laura. "This is who I go to. Actually, all of us, Caroline, Alabama, Cheyenne, Jessyka, Summer, and myself -all of us go to Dr. Hancock."

"What in the world would you guys need to see a

shrink for? You guys are normal." Laura looked shocked at Fiona.

"Joe never told you about what we went through?" Fiona asked shocked herself.

"He just said that he wanted me to meet you all that way when he was deployed again in the future, I had someone to talk to. Said that the men on the teams were just as overprotective of the women as he was of me, that was it."

Fiona lowered her head for a few moments and then looked up at Laura. "While I was on a couple of years ago, I was kidnapped and taken to Mexico by human traffickers." Laura gasped and sat back in her seat while Fiona continued her story. "I was beaten, raped, and drugged. I knew no one would have any reason to miss me because I had no family or any real friends in El Paso that I kept in touch with on a regular basis. I knew I wouldn't have anyone rescuing me. The only reason I was rescued was because Senator Lytle's daughter Julie was kidnapped by the same men. Being a Senator, the SEALs were called in. It was Hunter who rescued me from that nightmare in Mexico."

"I can see why they are as overprotective as they are then. This counselor that you see, how long did you see them before you started feeling safe again?

When were you ok with Cookie touching you intimately? I'm damaged Fiona. Mendoza broke me and doesn't even know it." Laura rambled out before breaking down and crying. Fiona got up from the chair and pulled Laura into her arms and held her while she cried.

"No, you're not damaged. You received a crack in your armor. You'll seal that crack again, Laura. You have me and Caroline. You've already met us. You'll be meeting the others when you're ready, and whether you realize it or not, you also have Matthew, my Hunter, especially Faulkner who asks about you all the time, Sam who does the same, Christopher, and Kason. You have all of them, just like you also have Joe and his entire team who would move heaven and earth to protect you. One day at a time, when you're ready, you'll know it. Joe isn't going anywhere. He loves you and will wait for you. He's like Hunter, alpha, overprotective, and willing to fight those demons for you and with you, if you let him. I know it doesn't feel like that right now because you're scared. But just take one day at a time. Talking to Dr. Hancock will help."

While Fiona and Laura were talking in the kitchen, there was a loud bang then an explosion outside. Both women jumped up and went to the window. Laura turned around and said urgently, "Fiona, go into my bedroom and hide in the closet. There's a safe for you to hide behind. Move some of the stuff to hide you. I made the space for Cody in case anyone was stupid enough to find me from some of our cases. Go now."

Laura ran to her room behind Fiona and got her weapon and ran back out to the living room. Fiona whispered out that she would call Cookie.

In the living room, Laura had her weapon in hand while she checked the doors and windows to make sure they were all locked. She set the alarm that way the alarm company would notify the police if they were breached. Suddenly, her front door blew off the hinge, knocking Laura back against the wall. When she woke up, her worst nightmare was standing in front of her with an evil grin on his face.

"Hola, senorita. Did you think I forgot about you? I wasn't done playing with you. It's very rude to run out on your host." Mendoza leaned down and pulled Laura up by her hair, smacking her across the face, and knocking her into the table. Mendoza looked over at the thug he brought with him and said, "Search the rest of the house, make sure there's no one else here."

Mendoza then grabbed Laura by the hair and

dragged her down the hall. He watched as his thug searched the hallway bathroom, Cody's room, the spare bedroom, and then followed him into Laura's room. He threw Laura onto the bed and started taking his jacket off. Laura jumped up when she saw the thug open the closet door and was ready to jump onto Mendoza to cause a distraction for Fiona to get out.

"House is clear. No one else is here. What do we do with her?"

"I'm going to have a little fun before we take her out of here. I'm going to keep her as my own personal toy. Time to remind her who the fucking boss is. Go into the living room and keep an eye out, make sure no one comes home expectantly. If they do, shoot them." As the thug left, Mendoza started unbuttoning his shirt, staring at Laura. "Do you seriously think you can fight me, senorita? I told you in Mexico you will never be rid of me."

"Fuck you, asshole. I will never stop fighting. Someone will always come looking for me. You'll never be able to sleep without one eye open wondering when they will strike."

Mendoza grabbed Laura and punched her hard in her stomach. Laura bowled over, grabbing her stomach at the same time she screamed out.

Mendoza then smacked her across the face knocking her to the floor. As Mendoza moved to straddle Laura, she kicked out, hitting him in the groin. They wrestled around on the floor fighting for control when Laura punched him in between the legs as hard as she could.

She heard shouts and shots ringing out in the living room as she dove for the open closet door. "Fiona, hand me the gun behind the safe!"

Laura felt Fiona place the gun in her hand and turned around at the same time Mendoza stood up and started to come at Laura and Fiona. Laura fired her weapon three times, hitting Mendoza all three times, two hitting his chest and one between the eyes, just like she was trained. Laura kept her gun raised as she stood up and slowly walked over to Mendoza to kick his leg. He was dead.

Laura looked up and ran to Fiona. "Oh my God, are you ok, Fiona?" Laura checked her over to make sure she wasn't hit or harmed in any way.

"Yes I'm good. Tex, Mendoza is dead. Laura just killed him. Where are the guys?"

Laura heard Tex's voice come through the phone, "They are there, they just breached the living room. Stay where you are and they will find their way to you. Are you both ok?

"Yes, Laura's more worried about me then she is herself."

All of the sudden there was noise in the hallway as Joe, Cookie, Dude, and Wolf breached the bedroom door with guns raised. They walked over to Mendoza lying on the ground and checked for a pulse. Satisfied he was dead, they looked to where Laura and Fiona sat huddled.

Joe ran over to Laura and pulled her into his arms while Cookie did the same with Fiona. "Are ye lasses ok?" Joe looked into Laura's eyes, noticing a fresh new bruise on her face. "Och love, if he wasn't already dead, I'd kill him myself. Are ye ok?" Joe kissed the bruise on her face.

Laura looked over at Cookie and Fiona and nodded. "Are you ok, Fiona? I'm sorry, so sorry. I never thought Mendoza would have come here. I'm sorry." Laura started crying.

Fiona broke away from Cookie and reached for Laura. "Hey, it's ok. I am fine. I called Tex when I couldn't get ahold of Cookie. Tex kept me calm the whole time telling me what was going on while he got ahold of them. I knew they were on the way. I was worried about you being out here." Fiona held Laura in her arms looking over Laura's head at Joe and Cookie.

———

JOE GOT Laura to the hospital to be checked out to make sure the assault didn't cause more injury or upset her old ones. When Joe tried to hold Laura's hand, she jerked her hand away from him. When the nurse left to get her discharge papers, Laura turned her head to Joe, "I'm going to stay at Dom's with Cody until I can get the door and windows fixed. I think it might be a good idea for you to go back to the base or stay with your brother for a few days."

"What do ye mean for me te stay at the base or a Marcu's? Lass, I'm nae leaving ye."

"Joe, please. Don't make this harder than it already is. This isn't going to work out, damn it. I'm poison to you, to your career, and to your friends. It was my fault Fiona was almost kidnapped or killed today. What the fuck do you think your friends would have thought of your girlfriend then? Huh? I can't do this anymore. I love you too damn much to ruin your career or turn your friends against you," Laura cried out.

Joe jumped up from his seat and grabbed Laura's shoulders, "Nae lass, ye are nae poison te me, my career, or my friends. Damn it, they were worried about ye too. Fiona was even worried about ye. They do nae think ye are poison. Do nae throw us away because of some trumped up idea that ye are saving me from some bullshite. I love ye. I'm nae giving ye up without a fight."

Laura struggled with Joe, crying, knocking his hands off of her. "It's over Joe. Please leave. I'm sorry, but I can't do this anymore. Please just go."

Joe stood up, looking at Laura like she'd lost her mind and slowly walked out of the room. He walked toward the waiting room, running into Dom. "Dom, take care of ye sister for me. I love her nae matter what she thinks. I'm nae giving up on her."

"Don't you dare give up on her. I know she loves you, too. Just give her time, Joe. You have my number. Give me a call when you get where you're going. I will take care of her. Just be patient, man. She's scared." Dom patted Joe's arm as he walked toward Laura's room.

Joe stood watching Dom walk toward the woman who held his heart. When Dom entered the room, Joe turned around and headed to the waiting room where Wolf and both teams waited for word. When he walked in, all he could do is stare at the room in a loss. He had his team, Wolf and his team, his brothers and his family back in Scotland, but he never felt so alone like he did right then and there.

"Hey man, is everything ok?" Wolf walked forward.

"She's going te her brother's for a few days until the door gets fixed. I'm going te get a hotel room for a few days. Let everyone know she's ok. She's being released here in a few."

"Wait, you're not staying with her at her brother's?" Wolf asked.

"Nae. She fucking ended things with us in that room. Some bullshite about her ruining my career or our friendship because she almost got Fiona killed. She thinks she's poison. That's her fucking demon of a mother talking. Damn it, man, I love her." Joe punched the wall startling everyone in the room.

"Hey, don't give up on her. She's scared right now. She doesn't really know how we are yet. We aren't giving up on her either. Just give her a few days to get herself put back together. Stay with me and Caroline. We have a room in the basement that you can use for a few days while you two get this figured out."

Joe sighed then nodded. "Aye man, I can do that.

I need te get some stuff from the house and make sure it's secure."

"Ok, we can take you there and help make sure the house is secure. It'll work out, Joe. I don't know how, but it will work itself out. You just hang in there and be patient."

11

Six days after Laura came home from the hospital, she reluctantly went to the house to make the arrangements to have the door and windows fixed. To her surprise, the door was replaced, as were the windows. Laura walked into the house and saw that the place had been cleaned up of all the damage and what needed to be fixed was fixed. There was no trace of what had happened. She found the card that Fiona had given her hanging on the fridge. She picked up the card and looked at it as tears started rolling down her face. She missed Joe like crazy. She wondered what he was doing, if he was ok, and if he missed her as much as she missed him. She didn't even know where he was staying.

She had gone back to work three days after the

attack and kept herself busy with going to work and taking care of Cody. She would go to work until Brocard sent her home, take care of Cody, and then clean Dom's apartment from top to bottom. She knew he was ready for her to go home. Having them there cut into his social life, but she just couldn't bring herself to go back to the house no matter what. Dom had come over and gotten her clothes, uniforms, and work gear. He tried to talk her into taking a few more days off work but she couldn't bring herself to do it.

She couldn't sleep at night because of the nightmares. Joe had helped her before whenever she had nightmares, now she felt so alone. It was her fault for ending things with Joe.

Laura walked into her bedroom and froze at the door. She was so surprised by what she saw, or rather what she didn't see. The room had been cleaned, sheets and bedspread had been changed and made up. There was a rose on the bed with a letter. Hesitantly, Laura walked over to the bed and picked up the rose and smelled it while picking up the letter.

My beautiful Laura

I KNOW you are not talking to me right now. I'm sure you're glad that at least my handwriting is in English since you joke that I speak a different language when I talk. Ah, there's my beautiful smile. I meant what I said in that hospital room, love - I'm not giving up on us. I love you, my beautiful heart. You're the Belle to my Beast, and the Beast is nothing without his Belle. I am here when you're ready, love. Just know that I am never far, I will dry your tears when you cry. I will hold you if you're scared. I will fight any demons that try to climb out of the dark into your beautiful light. I will slay the dragons that try to breathe fire and singe your beautiful skin. I will capture the wolves at the door and train them to be obedient guard dogs for their mistress. I will be that pillow you lay on when you're tired. You are my world, Laura Renee Pratt. You and our son Cody. I miss you both fiercely. I meant what I said a year ago love, Tha mi sa' ghaol leat Bidh gaol agam ort fad mo bheatha, thusa 's gun duine eile. I am in love with you, I will love you my whole life, you and no other. Never forget that, Laura.

I FIXED the door for you yesterday. Dom changed out the keys on your key ring so that you could get in. Wolf and the guys fixed the windows and helped clean up the mess. Caroline and the wives helped cleaned the house. I bought you a new bed, pillows, and linens.

I LOVE YOU LAURA.

Joe

LAURA SLID to the floor with her back to the dresser and cried. She just didn't know what to do. She loved him yet pushed him away out of fear. Laura pulled out her phone and called Caroline.

"Hello."

"Hi Caroline. It's Laura, I'm sorry to bother you, I'm sure I'm the last person you wanted to talk to right now. I was just wondering if you have seen Joe?"

"Laura, hi, how are you? Are you ok?"

"Yes. Sorry, I just saw Joe's note on the bed. I came to the house to make the arrangements to get things fixed. I wanted to thank you guys for all you've done."

"It was nothing, Laura. That's what friends are for. How are you?"

Laura sighed. "I'm ok."

"Laura, I can hear the sound of your voice. You've been crying. We are still having the cookout tomorrow. You better be here or I will come and get you myself."

Laura laughed. "I don't know yet, Caroline. How is Fiona? Is she doing ok?"

"Oh sweetie, she's fine. She's been worried about you just like we all have. Matthew and Hunter have threatened to hide our car keys if we didn't give you space." Caroline laughed.

"How is Joe?" Laura whispered.

"He is miserable without you. He's been sleeping in our basement instead of a hotel. The guys keep him occupied at night so he doesn't go to your brother's house and drag you out. He misses Cody. I think Dom let him call a few times to talk to Joe."

"He doesn't hate me?" Laura whispered.

"Oh Laura, *no*, he loves you. He knows you're hurting and he's had to fight not to crowd you. Come to the cookout tomorrow, Laura. I promise he will be happy to see you. Matthew and I will come pick you and Cody up or you can bring your brother with you. He's more than welcome to join us as well."

"I don't know. I'll let you know. Thank you, Caroline, I really appreciate it more than you know."

"Laura, call the number on the card that Fiona

gave you. I use Dr. Hancock also and can tell you that she's great. It won't happen overnight, but it does get better. Don't give up."

Laura hung up the phone and leaned her head back against the dresser with Caroline's words playing around in her head. She felt like she was damaged goods. She pulled the card out and looked at the number again. Picking up her phone she called Dr. Hancock. No more procrastination allowed.

———

THE NEXT MORNING, Laura drove down to the beach and watched the people walking and running in the sand. She walked down to the water and sat in the sand with her arms wrapped around her knees. Laura took her shoes off and put her toes out to be lapped at by the waves rolling in. She put her face up to the sky and breathed. She knew Caroline wanted her at the cookout, but she didn't know if she could be around everyone after she ended things with Joe.

On cue, her phone rang with the screen showing Caroline's number. "Hi Caroline, has Wolf had you tested for psychic abilities?"

"And give away my secrets? No, and don't you suggest it to him, either. Are you coming today?"

"I don't know if I can. Why do you want me there? I shut everyone out. I hurt Joe by ending things with him."

"Where are you, Laura?" Caroline requested, ignoring Laura's question.

Laura sighed knowing Caroline wouldn't give up. "I'm at the beach. I needed to get out away from everyone and everything and just think."

"Don't move. We will be there in a little bit." Caroline hung up.

"Caroline..." Laura was talking to dead air. "Well shit."

Thirty minutes later she felt Caroline sit down on one side of her then Fiona sat down on her other side. "You don't give anyone time, do you?" Laura chuckled.

"Technically we gave you a week to sulk and hide. Time's up." Fiona quipped. "Now to answer your question to Caroline, we both have told you that you're one of us. You're stuck with us, sister. No getting rid of us. Sorry Charlie. While your mouth may have told Joe things were over, your heart is telling you it isn't. You both took some time away from each other and that time is up. Joe is miserable without you, and you're miserable without him. I can see that just sitting here, so don't deny it. You have dark lines under your eyes, you look pale and probably haven't slept in that week either. Wolf, Dude, and Cookie are also waiting in the car to make sure you don't try to make a run for it."

"It's always the quiet ones you have to watch out for," Caroline joked. Laura and Fiona laughed.

"I called Dr. Hancock yesterday. They had a last-minute cancellation so I went for my first appointment. Thank you."

Fiona and Caroline leaned in and hugged Laura from each side. All of the sudden a shadow came over the girls. Laura looked up and saw her step-sister and her mother. Fiona looked back at Wolf, Cookie, and Dude while Laura and Caroline stood up.

"I didn't realize they allowed dogs on the beach," Jennifer snarked.

"Well, they allowed you in so I guess there's no guard to keep them out," Laura responded.

"You wish. Aren't you done being the family embarrassment? I heard Joe finally wised up and dumped your fat ass. Maybe I'll look him up now and show him what a real woman is like. I hear

SEALs know how to make a girl scream," Jennifer sneered at Laura.

"Well, I'm sure you can find some wanna-to-be SEALS, who might feel sorry for you. A real SEAL wouldn't touch a prostitute even if he was on his death bed," Carolina remarked. "And for your information, Joe didn't dump her. They are very much still together. You're just jealous because he chose the real woman and didn't look twice at you."

Jennifer looked behind the women and smiled big. "I guess we'll find out here shortly, won't we ladies? Look Mom, there are some fine specimens walking this way."

Laura looked behind her and saw Dude, Cookie, and Wolf walking toward them with hard looks on their faces.

"Jennifer, this isn't the time for you and Mom to cause a scene. Please just leave," Laura pleaded.

"Jesus Christ, Laura Renee. Where the hell did I go wrong with you? I gave birth to you, clothed you, put a roof over your head, and all you can do is embarrass this family. What did your father and I do to have you treat us this way? We found you someone who overlooked your weight and the fact you're a cripple. He treated you like gold and you divorced him because you couldn't do your wifely duties so he went outside the marriage bed. If you would just lose your weight, stop that ridiculous career you think you're doing good in, then you'll find a decent man. I'm sure Jonathan will even take you back. I don't understand why you can't see that we only mean well instead of assuming we're attacking you all the time. Seriously Laura, why do you have to make people think your family mistreats you?" Kathy complained.

"Probably because you do mistreat her. I don't know you from Adam, which is probably a good thing. And to answer your question ma'am, no we wouldn't touch you with a ten-foot pole or with a drug-addict-stoned-in-an-alley's dick. Joe and Laura have not broken up so you can get that out of your head. For you to think that a man should be ok to cheat on his wife because she doesn't conform to his ideals tells me all I need to know what kind of parent you are. Laura is loved by all of us. She has twelve new brothers and eight new sisters. She has a man who worships the ground she walks on. So, let me make this very clear, the three men you see standing right here, we are three of those new brothers in her life. You see her on the street, in a store, in a restaurant - I don't care where - you walk the other way. Do not approach her, do not contact her. She's no longer on your radar. Do you understand me?" Dude was pissed and let it be known what he'd witnessed

"Ugh whatever, you can have the loser." Jennifer and Kathy walked away.

"Now Laura, does that answer your question if these two didn't answer it already? You're one of us now. We look after our own. I meant what I told your mother and sister. Aside from Joe's team, you have this team and our wives. You even have Tex and Melody without even knowing it. You are not alone anymore. Are we clear?" Dude pulled Laura into his arms and hugged her. Wolf and Cookie took their turns hugging her as well.

Laura could only nod, overwhelmed by the show of support and love from her new family.

"Ok now that we have that out of the way. Can we please go back to the house where we have a cookout going full swing and put a very surly Scotsman out of his misery before these men drown him?" Caroline cracked.

Everyone laughed at Caroline's joke about Joe. "Are you sure?" Laura asked hesitantly.

Dude growled, "I'm going to kick your ass, woman. Let's go. We'll come back later for your car. You're not sneaking away." Dude threw his arm around Laura and made her walk with him.

12

Laura walked into the house with Caroline and Fiona on each side of her. Caroline kissed Wolf as he walked past her to go check on the backyard. Cookie did the same thing with Fiona and followed Wolf.

Dude stayed back, "Are you going to be ok?"

"Yeah, thanks, Dude. I'm just nervous. What if he's changed his mind?" Laura asked quietly.

"Then we'll kick his pansy ass and make it a party, SEAL style." Dude smirked.

Laura laughed at Dude's joke. She turned when she heard the back door opening and gasped when she saw Joe walk in. She squeezed Dude's hand once and walked over to Joe. She looked up into his eyes and held his gaze.

"Hi, lass. Wolf said ye were here. I had te see that

ye were ok myself." Joe had his hands in his front pockets to keep from reaching out for her.

"Hi, Joe. Is there someplace we can talk?"

"Aye we can go inte the kitchen or down te the basement where I've been sleeping."

Laura shrugged. "Either one's fine, lead the way."

Laura followed Joe down to the room in the basement. She put her hands in her front pockets mimicking Joe. She so badly wanted to reach out and touch him but she was so scared to do so. Instead she asked, "How are you?"

Joe looked at Laura like she'd grown an extra head. "How do ye think I am Laura? I am miserable without ye. I miss ye like crazy. I can't sleep at night since ye are nae next to me. I keep worrying about ye at night, wondering if ye are sleeping, if ye are eating, wondering if ye are ok with the nightmares. I've been in hell the last week, damn it."

"If it helps, I've been miserable, too. I miss you like crazy. I've missed having you hold me at night. I can't sleep. Captain Irby put me off yesterday, threatening to put me back on medical leave. Something about the walking dead weren't allowed in the office or she'd find someone to shove an arrow up my ass." Laura let out a small laugh.

Joe chuckled, "Sounds like ye Captain."

Laura sighed, "I called yesterday and made an appointment with Dr. Hancock -the shrink Fiona and Caroline recommended to me. They had a last-minute cancellation so I had my first appointment yesterday. I'll be seeing her twice a week for a couple of weeks."

Joe smiled at Laura. "I'm glad, love. What has Wolf, Cookie, and Dude in a snit when they came back from seeing ye at the beach?"

"Ah, you saw the looks, huh?" At Joe's nod Laura continued, "Apparently my mother and my step-sister Jennifer were at the beach walking and decided to make a scene. Dude lit into them both. He warned them that if they came near me they would regret it, something about twelve new brothers and eight new sisters."

Joe laughed at the image. "Aye, that would have been nice te see. Dude has a soft spot for women. He hates te see someone being put down. Apparently, his wife, Cheyenne, had the same kind of mother and sister. He can't stand that shite. But he's right, lass. Ye have my team, Doc's wife, Wolf's team, Tex, and their wives as family now."

"That's just it, Joe. I don't know why Wolf and his team are so overprotective of me like that. I ended things with you and yet they were still there helping you fix the chaos in the house. Technically, I should be the most hated female in the SEAL community right now."

Joe stepped forward and placed his hand on Laura's arm. "Lass, when these men found ye, ye held a gun te them, willing te still fight, even after they took out the men who were hurting ye. Ye put yourself in the line of fire when the arseholes came te harm those girls. Ye fought Mendoza with every breathe in ye body te keep those girls safe. Even injured ye walked four miles despite the pain ye were obviously in. Ye refused te allow the men te carry ye, afraid it would slow them down. When ye were shot, ye was nae the target, Wolf was. Ye stood up and turned at just the right time. Had ye just stood up, then ye would have been killed. But ye saved Wolf's life when ye stood up. Te these men, ye earned their respect because ye fought Laura. These men will also tell ye they have made mistakes with their lasses as well when they were going through what they were dealing with. But make nae mistake Laura, these men consider ye family and will come running if I'm nae here and ye need them. All ye would have te do is call them."

Laura could no longer hold in the tears. "I was so scared down there. I thought I would never see you again. Every time Mendoza would hit me, or whatever they would do, I kept thinking that was it. When Mendoza realized that he wasn't harming me or Cortez that way, he decided to get more aggressive with his beatings. He would tie Cortez into a chair and make her watch and then do the same to me. He would taunt us with hateful things. While we didn't give him what he wanted, I felt myself breaking. All I could think about was how you would look at me if you thought that Mendoza raped me. Would you still want me? Would you still love me? Could you still stomach to touch me, make love to me knowing that Mendoza had ruined me?" Laura broke down.

Joe pulled Laura into his arms. "Aye lass. I still want ye. I still love ye. I love ye more than I thought I could ever love someone. When ye are ready, yes, I will make love te ye. I will do everything in my power te erase him from ye memory. Ye are not ruined, damaged, or vile. Ye fought for the lives of four young girls. Ye made sure that they can have a normal life again and nae know the horrors that so many others have gone through. I'm nae going anywhere, lass. When ye are ready, I will be there for ye. I know Mendoza didn't rape ye, but ye still went through hell and back at that man's hands."

Laura laid her head on Joe's chest. "I want you to

come home with me now. I can't take one more night without you next to me. I can't fight these demons alone." Laura looked up at Joe, wrapping her arms around his neck, sliding her fingers up into his hair.

Laura pulled Joe's head down to hers. "Kiss me, Lt."

Joe gently placed his lips on her mouth and slowly teased her lips with his tongue before he started kissing her. He teased her with soft nips while enticing her tongue into a battle for control. He kept the kiss gentle, holding himself back, keeping his hands on her waist.

Laura could tell that Joe was holding back, afraid to scare her. "Damn it, I said kiss me. Please Joe, I need to know you still want me. I need to know that you still find me attractive."

"Fuck Laura, of course I still want ye. Aye lass, ye are the most attractive and most desirable woman on the planet. I don't want te scare ye if I make the wrong move. I would just as soon shoot myself in the arse than cause ye harm or fear."

Laura responded by pushing Joe and turned to walk away. "Just admit it, you look at me different now. I'll leave so I don't embarrass you with your friends."

Joe grabbed Laura, spun her around by the arm,

and slammed his lips down on hers, devouring her like a man starving for his last meal. He gripped her hair tight and backed her up against the wall. "I don't where ye think ye are going lass, but it sure as fuck is nae out that door. It's damn near killing me te keep my hands and mouth off of ye. I want te be balls deep in ye so fucking badly it hurts me much te hold back. But I know ye need time."

"No Joe, I need you. I'm tired of being afraid of my shadow, afraid of never feeling your touch, your heat. I'm so tired of wishing I could feel you inside me, but afraid that you'll think of Mendoza being there, get up and walk away and I'll never see you again."

Joe kissed Laura again, this time with more heat and hunger than she thought possible to feel in a kiss. His free hand went to her cheek to hold her in place as he ravished her lips. He fought her tongue for control, demanding control of the kiss, crushing her lips with his with each swipe.

Laura moved her hand from his neck down to his chest, undoing the buttons of his shirt one by one, removing his shirt from his jeans where it was tucked in. Once she had his shirt unbuttoned, she placed her hands on his chest, feeling his heart beating out of control just as hard and fast as hers. She lowered her hands slowly, inch by small inch to his taut stomach, feeling his six pack. She could feel her insides turning to mush. This is what she missed.

"Touch me, Joe, I need to feel your touch. Please," she whispered into his mouth, not wanting to break their kiss

Joe leaned back and looked into Laura's eyes and saw her pleading look. He moved back slightly to let his shirt fall to the floor, noticing the hunger in Laura's eyes as she looked at his chest and tattoos. She always did get hotter when she saw his tattoos. They were Laura's aphrodisiac, and she knew he loved every minute of it. He waited until her eyes were on his as he reached down and removed her shirt and felt his breathe catch. She felt so beautiful when he looked at her.

Joe leaned down and ran his tongue from her neck to the crook of her shoulder and back up. He nipped her ear gently as he kissed his way back down to her shoulder, slow and deliberate. One hand held her at the waist while his other hand went to her voluptuous breast he could feast on for days and still never have enough. He pulled the cups of her bra down causing her breasts to pop out, lifting them up like an offering on the alter he gladly accepted.

Laura leaned her head back against the wall as he moved his mouth from her shoulder down to her breast, licking, sucking, teasing, nipping, and making a meal out of her. Laura moaned as he felt his mouth tasting her. She moved her hands from his waist down to the buttons of his jeans, working them open. Once she got his jeans open, she reached in and found him hard as steel and ready to blow.

She stroked him slowly, up and down as she moaned from his mouth on her nipple. She felt his hands move from her waist down to her jeans, opening the buttons, and then his hands sliding inside. Laura tensed at first, stopping her movement, removing her hand.

"It's just me, lass. I'll stop. I'm sorry I don't mean te go te fast."

"No, it's ok. Just talk to me. I need to hear your voice, Joe. Please don't stop."

"Aye lass, are ye sure? I don't want te scare ye."

Laura reached for his hardness and started stroking him again, slowly as she looked into his eyes. "I want you inside me now, Lt."

Joe stared at Laura to make sure she was serious. In that moment, Laura decided to take matters into her own hands. She removed her hands from his hardness and pushed him away from her. She grabbed the top of her jeans and shoved them down her legs, underwear and all. She walked toward him, grasping the top of his jeans shoving them down his legs, then going back up and grabbing the waist of his underwear and pulling them down, freeing his cock for her touch. She went down to her knees, taking him into her hands, teasing the tip with her tongue as she looked up into his eyes.

Laura took his cock into her mouth, as far as he would go, licking and sucking him. She teased the tip just a little with her mouth then took him fully in, never breaking eye contact.

Joe leaned down and pulled her up, "Ack lass, ye know I won't last when ye are doing that."

Joe pushed Laura back up against the wall, grabbing her leg to wrap around his waist. Reaching between them, he tested to make sure she was ready for him. He found her soaking his fingers as he touched her clit, teasing the bundle of nerves.

"Ah my bonnie lass, ye are so fucking wet. I want ye taste on my tongue, but I can't last much longer. I promise te make it up te ye tonight if ye will have me."

"Yes, make it up to me later but for the love of

God, please don't make me wait any longer. I need you." Laura gripped Joe's hair and pulled him down for a heated kiss as she bucked her hips trying to find his hardness to impale her.

Joe gripped Laura's waist, lifting her slightly, letting his cock seek her wetness as she leaned against the wall. Laura squeezed her legs against his waist pulling him into her then lowering herself onto his cock to the hilt. She gasped as she felt him fill her. She would never get over how he filled her so completely. It was always a tight fit when he took her and she loved the feeling, no matter how uncomfortable it felt at first, she could never get enough of him.

Joe froze, giving her a moment to adjust. She was sure he was worried about her reaction, too. When he realized she wasn't going to panic and push away, he started moving in and out of her heat. Slowly, oh so annoyingly slow.

"Joe, if you don't start fucking me within an inch of my life, I will cut you in your sleep."

"Ah lass, ye are so violent. I love ye, either way. I want this to last, but ye have me on the edge, love."

Laura used the heels of her feet to press into his ass to get him to move. Joe growled as he looked into her eyes and started moving faster. He gripped her waist in one hand, with the other hand holding braced against the wall, and set a harder and faster pace. Laura gasped as she felt him moving in and out of her, harder and faster, relishing the feel of him owning her. She growled as she felt her climax rising fast and hot.

"Don't stop. Fuck, I love it when you're inside me. Oh God, yes!" Laura reached between them and touched her clit and rubbed twice, sending her climax through the roof. Leaning forward, she bit Joe on the shoulder to hold the scream back.

As Laura's teeth sank into his shoulder at the same time her heat gripped him tightly, Joe lost his control. Two more pushes and he roared his climax. He emptied himself inside her, holding himself deep inside. He leaned over and kissed her lips.

"Fuck, lass. I've missed ye so much. I love ye."

Laura peppered Joe's lips with small kisses. "I love you, too. I've missed you more than you realize. I'm sorry I was such a bitch and pushed you away. I was scared of embarrassing you. Fiona had just told me about her past when Mendoza attacked, all I could think about was them hating me because I caused her to relapse. I didn't want to cause you trouble. Can you forgive me?"

"Aye lass, there is nothing to forgive. I understand why you were upset and afraid. So do Fiona and Caroline. Cookie wanted to come and tell you himself along with Fiona, but Dom felt you needed more time. I can see he was right. If we'd come over the next day it would have pushed you further away. It has to be in your time."

"Yeah well, you fuckers know how slow I am with this crap. Just don't give up on me. I am sure I will have back slides. Dr. Hancock even said so. Just don't give up on me Joe, that's all I ask."

"Never, lass. There's twelve men who would have my arse and bury me in a desert if I ever did such a stupid thing. Ye couldn't get rid of me if ye tried."

There was a knock before they heard the door open. "Are you two alive down here?"

Joe and Laura laughed at Caroline's question. "Yes Caroline, we're alive. We'll be up in just a few minutes."

13

Joe and Laura rejoined the group upstairs after getting cleaned up. When they walked outside to the party, they were greeted by cheers and catcalls. Laura hung her head as Joe pulled her into his arms and flipped his teammates and friends off with a shit-eating grin on his face.

"Please for the love of all that is holy, tell us that you have put us out of our misery or am I going to have to curse your name for longer because he's going to continue to kick our ass in training?" Mac joked as he came up to hug Laura.

Laura laughed as she hugged Mac back. "Eh, I guess I can take his ornery ass back. Fucker still owes me a Star Wars and Lethal Weapons marathon."

Everyone around the group laughed. Cookie walked forward and pulled Laura into his arms, hugging her. "You're one of ours, Laura. I know you blamed yourself for Mendoza showing up at the house while Fiona was there. But you did everything you could to protect her. You made sure she was safe, no matter what happened to you. To me, that's a huge plus in my book because you didn't hesitate, you acted. Fiona is ok and was more worried about you than she was for herself this last week. We all wanted to come to you and assure you that no one held any ill will or blamed you for what happened, but we also knew that had we done that, it would have pushed you further away. You have us in your corner, come hell or high water. You're stuck with us. Don't make me prove it, Cookie style." Cookie winked at Laura as he stepped away after giving her another hug.

Laura laughed at the description that Cookie painted. "Thank you."

Each man came up and hugged her, leaving Dude for last with Wolf and Joe standing next to him. "By now you've heard what we've all had to say. You're one of us. I meant every word I said to your mother and your sister. All you have to do is call and we are there, no questions or hesitations."

Dude looked up at Dom who had walked up to stand behind his sister along with Cody while Cookie had been giving his speech. "That goes for you, as well. We may not know you from Adam, but you're one of us. Treat this gift with respect and love her like we all do, and you'll always have us at your back."

Dude got down on one knee so he was on Cody's level. "Same goes for you, squirt. You ever need anything, you can come to us and we'll be there. You have twelve new uncles and eight new aunts who will move heaven and earth to be there for you. Be there to cheer you on and help you with whatever you need. Except math, we give that to Benny since he's the girl in the kitchen."

"Hey, that's not funny, asshole." Benny laughed at Dude's joke. "But he's right, I can help you with math."

"Sure about that, Benny? Well ye do know ye multiplications, apparently with the little ones running around," Joe quipped.

Benny flipped Joe off and winked at Laura and Cody. Caroline came forward and handed Joe a box. Laura looked from the two quizzically and kind of scared. "That's not going to explode, is it?"

Before Laura realized what was going on, Joe got

down on one knee in front of everyone at the cook-out. "Are you ok? Did you hurt yourself?"

Wolf and Dude snickered behind Laura as Joe shot them an evil glare. "Nae, lass. I'm not hurt." Joe took a deep breath and let it out.

"Laura Renee Pratt, ye are my everything. In the year we've been together, every day I fall in love with ye even more. Ye smile is the first thing I long te see in the morning. Hearing ye soft snore at night, knowing ye are next to me," Joe chuckled as Laura flipped him off for saying she snores. "Aye love ye do snore, that's how I know I am home with ye. I never thought I'd settle for one woman or want te be a father with my career. But this past year with ye and Cody has made me realize I didn't know what a dumbarse I was in that thinking. Now I can't imagine my life without ye two. I can't wait for my day to end at work so that I can get home te ye both."

"Jesus Christ man, just fucking bloody ask her already. Mum will be old and wrinkled by the time ye damn speech is made."

Joe glared at the man who spoke up, flipping him off to the chuckles of everyone in the crowd then he turned back around to Laura. "Before the arseoff coo of a brother interrupted, Laura Renee Pratt, would ye do me the honor of wearing my grandmother's ring and becoming my wife?"

Joe opened the box, took the ring, and placed it on her ring finger as he stared up at her.

Laura kept staring at the ring with tears streaming down her face. Her son Cody leaned into her and whispered "Um mom, I think he's waiting for an answer. Can he be my dad?"

Everyone laughed at Cody's attempt of being quiet. Laura looked at Joe and nodded her head, "Aye, I'll marry you."

Everyone cheered as Joe picked her up and spun her around as he kissed her. "About bloody fucking time. Mum has been blowing up my phone asking if the daft arse has asked her yet."

Laura looked at the voice and laughed. Running into Joe's younger brother Marcus' arms to hug and kiss him. "Says the man who's being the bigger jackass instead of making the move on a woman he's been drooling after for a year now."

After teasing Marcus, Laura went back to Joe and wrapped her arms around his midsection and looked up into his eyes. She was finally home.

SCOTTISH GLOSSARY:

As most of you have probably figured out, Joe is Scottish. I have included a small glossary so that you can understand what he is saying when he talks.

nae - not

te - to

ye - ye

dinnae - don't

coo - cow

ken - know

mannie - boy

lass - lady

mum - mom

arse - ass

croie - heart

cannae - can not

aye – yes

Joe also speaks Gaelic to Laura a few times. I have included the words here for better understanding.

Tha mi sa' ghaol leat

Bidh gaol agam ort fad mo bheatha, thusa 's gun duine eile

I am in love with you, I will love you my whole life, you and no other.

mo chridhe croie- my heart and soulmate

Gradh mo Chridh - love of my heart

tha goal agam ort - I love you

Author Bio:

KD Michaels has lived all over the country pretty much thanks to her nomadic ways. Being born a military brat but unable to join the military herself due to her deafness, she gave in to her inherited love of travel and has no problems picking up and throwing a bag in the car with one of her kids and just going where the wind blows her. She hails originally from North Carolina, but has lived in Arizona for the longest, working in law enforcement there before going back to North Carolina to be with family. She now lives in Virginia Beach where she caves to her love of the ocean and the wind in her hair. She's a mom to three and a cat which talks back and thinks he's a dog when he wants to cuddle.

To connect with KD Michaels, go to her Facebook page at: https://www.facebook.com/authorkd.michaels

Her Guardian of Hope Series page: https://www.facebook.com/Guardians-of-Hope-Series-1604509269791748/?ref=aymt_homepage_panel

Her Twitter page: https://twitter.com/azcrimegrl

OTHER BOOKS BY KD MICHAELS

Special Forces: Operation Alpha

Saving Laura

Protecting Shane

Guardians of Hope Series

Angel of Horror

Standalone

Montana Gypsy

ABOUT THE AUTHOR

KD Michaels has lived all over the country pretty much thanks to her nomadic ways. Being born a military brat but unable to join the military herself due to her deafness, she gave in to her inherited love of travel and has no problems picking up and throwing a bag in the car with one of her kids and just going where the wind blows her. She hails originally from North Carolina, but has lived in Arizona for the longest, working in law enforcement there before going back to North Carolina to be with family. She now lives in Virginia Beach where she caves to her love of the ocean and the wind in her hair. She's a mom to three and a cat which talks back and thinks he's a dog when he wants to cuddle.

To connect with KD Michaels, go to her Facebook page   at:
https://www.facebook.com/authorkd.michaels

Her   Guardian   of   Hope   Series   page:

https://www.facebook.com/Guardians-of-Hope-Series-1604509269791748/?ref=aymt_homepage_panel

Her Twitter page: https://twitter.com/azcrimegrl

facebook.com/authorkd.michaels

Liz Crowe: Marking Mariah

Jordan Dane: Redemption for Avery

Jordan Dane: Fiona's Salvation

Riley Edwards: Protecting Olivia

Riley Edwards: Redeeming Violet

Nicole Flockton: Protecting Maria

Nicole Flockton: Guarding Erin

Nicole Flockton: Guarding Suzie

Nicole Flockton: Guarding Brielle

Casey Hagen: Shielding Nebraska

Casey Hagen: Shielding Harlow

Casey Hagen: Shielding Josie

Desiree Holt: Protecting Maddie

Kathy Ivan: Saving Sarah

Kathy Ivan: Saving Savannah

Kathy Ivan: Saving Stephanie

Jesse Jacobson: Protecting Honor

Jesse Jacobson: Fighting for Honor

Jesse Jacobson: Defending Honor

Jesse Jacobson: Summer Breeze

Silver James: Rescue Moon

Silver James: SEAL Moon

Silver James: Assassin's Moon

Becca Jameson: Saving Sofia

Kate Kinsley: Protecting Ava

Heather Long: Securing Arizona

MJ Nightingale: Protecting Secrets

Sarah O'Rourke: Saving Liberty

Debra Parmley: Protecting Pippa

Lainey Reese: Protecting New York

Jenika Snow: Protecting Lily

Jen Talty: Burning Desire

Jen Talty: Burning Kiss

Jen Talty: Burning Skies

Jen Talty: Burning Lies

Megan Vernon: Protecting Us

Megan Vernon: Protecting Earth

As you know, this book included at least one character from Susan Stoker's books. To check out more, see below.

Delta Force Heroes Series

Rescuing Rayne (FREE!)

Rescuing Aimee (novella)

Rescuing Emily

Rescuing Harley

Marrying Emily

Rescuing Kassie

Rescuing Bryn

Rescuing Casey

Rescuing Sadie

Rescuing Wendy

Rescuing Mary (Oct 2018)

Rescuing Macie (April 2019)

Badge of Honor: Texas Heroes Series

Justice for Mackenzie (FREE!)

Justice for Mickie

Justice for Corrie

Justice for Laine (novella)

Shelter for Elizabeth

Justice for Boone

Shelter for Adeline
Shelter for Sophie
Justice for Erin
Justice for Milena
Shelter for Blythe
Justice for Hope (Sept 2018)
Shelter for Quinn (Feb 2019)
Shelter for Koren (June 2019)
Shelter for Penelope (Oct 2019)

SEAL of Protection Series

Protecting Caroline (FREE!)
Protecting Alabama
Protecting Fiona
Marrying Caroline (novella)
Protecting Summer
Protecting Cheyenne
Protecting Jessyka
Protecting Julie (novella)
Protecting Melody
Protecting the Future
Protecting Kiera (novella)
Protecting Dakota

SEAL of Protection: Legacy Series

Securing Caite (Jan 2019)

Securing Sidney (May 2019)
Securing Piper (Sept 2019)
Securing Zoey (TBA)
Securing Avery (TBA)
Securing Kalee (TBA)

New York Times, *USA Today* and *Wall Street Journal* Bestselling Author Susan Stoker has a heart as big as the state of Texas where she lives, but this all American girl has also spent the last fourteen years living in Missouri, California, Colorado, and Indiana. She's married to a retired Army man who now gets to follow *her* around the country.

She debuted her first series in 2014 and quickly followed that up with the SEAL of Protection Series, which solidified her love of writing and creating stories readers can get lost in.

If you enjoyed this book, or any book, please consider leaving a review. It's appreciated by authors more than you'll know.

www.stokeraces.com
www.AcesPress.com
susan@stokeraces.com

Made in the USA
Middletown, DE
24 November 2018